NICK COURAGE

DELACORTE PRESS

rhcbooks.com

Educators and librarians, for a variety of teaching tools, visit us at RHTeachersLibrarians.com

Library of Congress Cataloging-in-Publication Data
Names: Courage, Nick, author.
Title: Storm blown / Nick Courage.
Description: First edition. | New York : Delacorte Press, [2019] | Summary: In San Juan, Puerto Rico, Alejandro worries about his great-uncle while helping guests at a resort, and in New Orleans, Emily worries about her sick brother, as a major hurricane rages, changing both their lives forever.
Identifiers: LCCN 2018018885 | ISBN 978-0-525-64596-2 (hc) | ISBN 978-0-525-64599-3 (glb) | ISBN 978-0-525-64597-9 (ebook)
Subjects: | CYAC: Hurricanes—Fiction. | Refugees—Fiction. | Survival—Fiction. | Puerto Rico—Fiction. | New Orleans (La.)—Fiction.
Classification: LCC PZ7.1.C677 Sto 2019 | DDC [Fic]—dc23

The text of this book is set in 12-point Mercury Text G2.
Interior design by Ken Crossland

Printed in the United States of America
10 9 8 7 6 5 4 3 2 1
First Edition

For anyone who's ever weathered a storm.

But for Rachel, especially.

During major storms, sea birds and waterfowl
are most exposed. . . . In a unique effect of
cyclonic hurricanes, the eye of the storm with
its fast-moving walls of intense wind can form
a massive "bird cage" holding birds inside the
eye until the storm dissipates.

—National Wildlife Federation,
"Seven Things to Know About How
Hurricanes Affect Wildlife"

PART ONE

HATCHING

When the first glimpse of day appears, I make
my way on deck, where I stand not unlike a
newly hatched bird, tottering on feeble legs.

—JOHN JAMES AUDUBON, *BIRDS OF AMERICA*,
VOLUME VII, "WILSON'S PETREL"

SAN JUAN, PUERTO RICO

JUNE 10—11:00 A.M.

"Alejandro!" the old man shouted, his voice small in the rising wind. *"Las sillas*—the chairs, they're blowing away!"

A turquoise lounger slid across the slick deck of the San Juan Pilastro Resort and Casino, its waterproof fabric stretched and filled like the sails of a ship. Alejandro ran after it, his skinny shoulders squared against the wind and rain as his *padrino* squinted at the approaching storm. Most of the guests had already evacuated, cutting their vacations short as weather advisories rolled in with the clouds. The few who had hoped for the best and ignored the warnings were holed up in their rooms, enjoying complimentary cocktails and wondering if it was too late to leave.

It *was* too late.

Just minutes before, Alejo and his mother's uncle—Padrino Nando—had joined the hotel staff in the lobby for an emergency meeting. They'd stood near the doors with the other groundskeepers, not wanting to track mud onto the marble floors as the manager informed them that the bad weather they'd been having all week had been upgraded to a tropical storm.

Tropical Storm Valerie.

Nando had laughed and clapped his hands.

It was a name like one of their tourists, another Hawaiian-shirted guest with no real love for the island. But Valerie was nothing to laugh about—all flights out of Isla Verde were grounded until the storm blew over, and most of the birds were already gone. The loons, the geese, the herons, and even the gulls—they were smart like that. Except for a handful of purple-black cormorants that were fighting the wind for fun, the swirling gray skies were empty.

Padrino Nando smiled as Alejandro dragged the runaway lounger back to the others, tying them all down with a bright nylon rope. Somewhere in the Atlantic Ocean, not so very far from shore, winds were gusting over forty miles per hour. "Faster than traffic," their manager had said. Sometime that night or the following morning, those winds and the rain would hit San Juan and the streets would flood and end the tourist season early.

Or everything would be fine.

It all depended on how angry the white peaks were, out in the surf.

"Alejo!" Nando shouted. "Look!"

The palm trees lining the Pilastro's white sand beach bent toward the resort, their leafy crowns catching the wind. Beyond them, the cormorants took turns dive-bombing the roiling white waves. With the sky so gray and the sea so gray and the rain running down their faces, it was hard to tell what was earth and what was air.

Nando squeezed Alejo's shoulder with one wrinkled hand as they watched the cormorants fish, shading his eyes with the other to better see their long necks piercing the surf like arrows from the heavens. No matter what happened, the storm would be gone in a few days—spinning up to Bermuda or threading its way into the Gulf of Mexico, toward the oil rigs and refineries off the muddy coasts of Louisiana and Texas.

Padrino Nando didn't care where the storm went, only that the cormorants were full and happy.

As long as there were birds in the waves, San Juan would be fine.

NEW ORLEANS

JUNE 10—2:00 P.M.

By the time Sam Gribley developed a taste for frog soup, Emily had finally settled into her book. It hadn't been easy. Sam's story was written so long ago that Emily was borrowing her mom's childhood copy of *My Side of the Mountain*. They'd both had it assigned for summer reading, twenty years apart, and the pages were brittle and yellow. Emily traced her finger over an ancient crease, her vision blurring at the edges as she folded and unfolded the same corner her mother had dog-eared when she was a kid. She tried not to think about Elliot and the surgery, and her dad working on the oil rig while her mom worried herself sick . . . but it was all too much.

She couldn't concentrate.

The words just wouldn't stick in her head.

It didn't help that their apartment was so small.

Between the low groan of Elliot's humidifier and the cable news blasting from the living room, she'd had to stop three times and start from the beginning. The thought of starting all over again was too much for Emily to bear, so she chewed her lip and turned the page. Sam— the main character—had run away from home and was camping in a hollowed-out tree . . . but Emily had to admit that he was doing okay for himself.

Maybe even better than she was.

Emily had been living on fast food for the past month, and her mouth watered as she reread the recipe for Sam's favorite meal: acorn flour, water-lily buds, and wild onions served in a polished turtle-shell bowl. If you left out the frog legs, it'd be perfect . . . but even without them, there was no way she could get any of that stuff at their grocery store. The Winn-Dixie they went to on Saturday mornings had flickering fluorescent lights and a security guard who was always sipping from a quart of pink, flavored milk.

It wasn't a farmer's market, that was for sure.

Emily's mom cursed at the news while Emily day-dreamed about handpicked mussels sizzling over an open fire and the crunch of fresh green vegetables. Soon they'd start shopping at the fancy stores again, the ones they'd gone to before Elliot got sick.

The ones where happy people got their groceries.

Those stores had *everything*.

For the fourth time that morning, Emily closed her book, holding her place with a finger. It was too hard to stay focused while she was blinking back tears. "I'm fine," she whispered, but the tremble in her voice gave her away. Even though everyone said Elliot was going to be fine, Emily felt sad—and the apartment was dark and cold, which made her sadness feel more real.

For the past week, the curtains had been pulled tight to keep out the dust, for Elliot. Before he came home from the hospital, Emily and her mother had scrubbed the apartment on their hands and knees until everything smelled like lemon and bleach, and then the real cleaners had come. Another mother and daughter team. They'd turned the radio up so loud it drowned out the television and they'd sung along to songs Emily recognized from the aisles at the grocery store.

It had felt good to have them in the apartment, laughing and singing in the warm, late afternoon light.

It felt like a new start.

Emily's mom had smiled then, and Emily had smiled, too.

Before the cleaners, the entire summer had felt wrong.

As soon as school had let out, most of Emily's friends had gone straight into summer camp. The others had left on long road trips to ramshackle cabins and rented beach houses in Pensacola, like her friend Katie. One girl was going to Mexico to see the pyramids. Emily knew because they'd all had to write essays about their summer plans and read them out loud to the class. Emily had written about visiting her aunt Lillian in Florida. She was proud of her essay. Aunt Lillian had promised to take her to a clear-water swimming hole where you had to keep an eye out for alligators. Everyone thought that was a lie, but it wasn't.

Except that she never got to go to Florida after all.

Emily frowned.

So far, she had spent most of her summer curled up on two hard plastic chairs in the hospital waiting room listening to her mom whisper-shout at the insurance companies, Aunt Lillian, Emily's dad, and whoever else Emily's mom could get on the phone. Emily's friends texted her inside jokes and photos of themselves buried in sand. Emily always responded, but her heart wasn't in it. Most of them didn't know about Elliot, and she didn't know how to tell them.

While Emily's mom watched the never-ending news in their dark and disinfected apartment, Emily listened to children playing in their shared backyard. The world was full of people who didn't know what they were going through.

Normal people.

Her tears were slow and hot, and she bravely sniffed them back as her book slipped loudly to the floor.

"Emily!" her mom shouted from the living room.

Emily waited for footsteps—but none came. Her mother was planted firmly on the couch, watching the weekend weather forecast. As usual. Emily closed her eyes and pictured her staring, moonfaced, at the glowing blue screen.

"Em, are you okay?"

"I'm fine," Emily shouted, forcing herself to smile so she might actually *sound* fine. She rubbed the tears from her eyes with the back of her hand and kept the smile plastered to her face.

There was no way they could have known that everything would be even harder when Elliot came home. He had always been thin, but he was so much thinner when he was released from the hospital. His dirty blond hair looked brown and his lips were cracked. The nurses had joked that he got a little dinged up in the shop and Emily's mom had laughed gratefully, like it was the funniest thing she'd ever heard . . . but when they got Elliot back into his bedroom, she was so scared he would get sick again that Emily wasn't even allowed to see him, even though her hands still smelled like lemons.

Even though Elliot had been her best friend since the day she was born.

Emily picked her mother's book up from the floor, smoothing the pages where they had crumpled. "I'm going outside," she said to no one in particular. She slipped her phone into her pocket and walked to Elliot's room. The doorknob felt cold in her hand. Refreshing. She half turned it, then stopped. If there had been a sliver of light, she would have gone in, but the crack beneath the door was dark, as usual, and there wasn't any point in getting their mom worked up. The floorboards creaked as she tiptoed away, so loudly that she almost didn't hear her brother calling her name from the shadows.

NEW ORLEANS

JUNE 10—2:10 P.M.

Elliot rubbed the sleep from his eyes as his sister ducked into his bedroom. It hurt to sit up, but he sat up anyway. The stitches crisscrossing his stomach felt tight—so tight that he was worried they might pop—but Elliot clenched his teeth and tried to ignore the pain as a stack of comic books slipped and fluttered from his mattress onto the floor. His mom had arranged them next to him while he slept, hoping he'd wake up well enough to read.

But he was always so groggy.

It was the medicine.

The pain pills made it so he couldn't stay up for more than a few hours at a time. And even when he wasn't sleeping, he wasn't quite awake. It felt like he was floating underwater. Like the voices on the street outside his window were from another world, a hundred miles away.

Elliot sighed as his sister tiptoed through the darkness.

In school, he was always getting in trouble for not sitting still. If his homeroom teacher could see him now, he thought, she wouldn't believe her eyes. It had been over a week since he'd worn shoes—and it was getting harder to remember a time when he could jump around "creating an environment of total chaos, to the detriment of his teachers and classmates."

That was what his last progress report had said.

He'd never forget his mother reading that line out loud at the dining room table—so shocked and exasperated—while Emily laughed into her peas and their dad tried to hide a smile behind a forkful of mashed potatoes.

These days, Elliot wasn't even sure where his shoes *were*.

"Hey," he said. "Emily?"

His voice cracked, and he cleared his throat. It was a waste of a summer vacation: lying in bed, alone, in the dark. He was so sick of it he could scream. Instead, he tried to arrange a smile on his face for his little sister, like nothing was wrong.

Like he was fine.

It wasn't so hard to do, even with the stitches pulling on his side.

There was something about the way Emily was sneaking toward his bed, like a ninja, that made the corners of his mouth twitch upward. He would have laughed, but even in the low light of his bedroom he could see that her cheeks were wet with tears. "What's wrong?" he whispered, but Emily put a finger to her lips and held it there for a long moment, waiting for the creak of a floorboard to recede.

"Mom won't let me in here," she finally said, when she was sure that their mother wasn't coming. Her voice was so soft that Elliot had to strain to hear her over the sound of the television in the living room, and she kept looking over her shoulder in terror, like she might dive under his bed any second.

Elliot felt his smile widen.

It wasn't funny—not "ha ha" funny—but Emily looked so serious that Elliot couldn't help it. The stitches stretched and pulled as he started to laugh, and the pain was immediate—a flash of red that took his breath away as he fell back down onto his pillow. Emily stared at him from the shadows, her eyes wide as Elliot clutched his side.

"I'm okay," he said, his voice ragged as his pulse pounded in his temples.

Even with his eyes closed, he could feel his sister staring at him.

Worrying.

"It's not *you*," he sighed, breaking the silence. "Mom's just scared, is all."

Emily didn't answer.

They both knew it was an understatement.

You didn't have to be a genius to see that their mom was so scared that she wasn't herself anymore. Even half-conscious on his bed, Elliot could sense the change in the apartment. The *stress.* He told himself that once their dad came back, everything would be different. That their mom would be able to put down the Purell and relax again. Until then, though, it was up to Elliot to help his little sister get through the weirdness.

"I'm gonna be okay," he said. "You know that, right?"

Emily shrugged.

"I just wish things were normal again," she whispered. "You know?"

It was easier for him, Elliot realized, sleeping in his room all day. Waited on hand and foot while his sister tiptoed around the house. Dealing with their mother. He watched Emily jump at the sound of the television from the living room and sighed. "Normal is boring," he finally said. "When I get better, I'm never gonna be bored again."

Emily smiled, which only made her look sadder.

"Seriously," Elliot said. "When I get out of this bed, I'm not getting back in it. Even when Dad's here and everything's back to normal. I'll camp out in the park if I have to. You can come visit me on that little island, with the birds."

Emily smiled again, with her eyes this time.

The island in Audubon Park was a small, ragged clump of cattails and goose poop in the middle of a shallow lagoon. It was only sixty feet out from shore, but neither Emily nor Elliot had ever been there. To get to it, you'd have to wade through the muck and mud—in front of everyone—and there wasn't any reason to do that, even though they'd talked about it since they were little.

"Emily!"

Elliot watched his sister cringe as their mom shouted from down the hall. "Everything's gonna be okay," he said, squeezing her wrist before she slouched back into the living room—the weight of the world on her shoulders. Before she could close the door behind her, he heard his mother reprimanding her.

"You can't be in there," she said, her voice high and sharp. "You *know* that."

Elliot took a deep breath, filling his lungs.

Feeling his stitches stretch and pull.

He didn't like the way his mom was acting. That she was making his sister so sad. But his eyelids were heavy. *So heavy*. And there was nothing he could do about it, not before their dad came home. The sound of the television and the traffic on the avenue blurred together and receded into the distance as Elliot drifted back to sleep, the smell of hand sanitizer and antiseptic wipes hanging like a fog above his clouded head.

SAN JUAN, PUERTO RICO

JUNE 10—4:00 P.M.

It had been hours since Padrino Nando had clocked out.

He'd driven his salt-rusted yellow truck back to La Perla, windshield wipers cranking against the rain as he raced home to shutter his windows before the storm. But Alejo was still at the San Juan Pilastro Resort and Casino. Not wanting to miss the excitement, he had waved goodbye as Nando pulled out of the mostly empty garage—then raced back inside, where the hotel staff had gathered. Tropical Storm Valerie was coming, and the televisions in the resort's marble-tiled lobby were saying that she could be *la tormenta del siglo.*

The storm of the century.

They'd watched the news reports—frozen in front

of the television screens—until the Pilastro's manager blew in from the back deck, tucking her windswept hair behind her ears. She'd called an emergency meeting—right there, in the lobby—to run through a preparedness checklist. Afterward, Alejo sprinted from room to room, helping the last remaining guests pull their thick blue curtains closed. This was necessary, the manager had explained, to protect the guests from broken glass, should Valerie come knocking at their windows.

Everyone was laughing and breathless, giddy at the thought of danger.

To the guests, it was like a fire drill . . . without the annoying alarms.

"It's nothing," Alejo had said over and over again, in countless identical rooms.

But in between suites, the hallways felt eerily abandoned.

The hotel had more or less emptied at the first sign of danger. Eighty percent of its occupants had packed up their suitcases to brave the crowds at Luis Muñoz Marín International Airport, but the San Juan Pilastro was a sprawling resort. Dozens of guests were still huddled around their televisions, their complimentary-breakfast trays sitting like distress signals on the thick turquoise carpeting in front of their rooms.

Those were the doors Alejo had to knock on.

Those were the guests he'd been asked to reassure.

Over time he developed a system, like a game.

"It's nothing." He would smile as he pulled the curtains closed. "It really is nothing," he would repeat, and the guests—all foreigners trapped on vacation—would smile weakly back at him, wishing they had left while they still could. Then Alejo would hold up his hands, apologizing for the inconvenience. "In San Juan," he would say, "this happens every year, all the time—and we're still here!"

The manager had told them to say this, and it worked. Most of the remaining guests called down for their complimentary cocktails before he even left their rooms, laughing at their own bad luck. The hotel bar made so many Dark 'n' Stormies that they ran out of rum halfway through Alejo's rounds, switching to something they were calling a Frozen Valerie. It was sweet and cold and green, and they were making it by the bucket in the kitchen.

"We have to keep them calm," his manager had said, her hands on her hips, a general addressing her troops. "Valerie we can live through, but bad reviews . . ."

She left her sentence hanging, as if it were too unthinkable to even finish.

Alejo bounced on the balls of his feet, vibrating with nervous energy.

He loved his summers at the Pilastro.

He loved the pool and the beach and tagging along with his *padrino,* who gave Alejo an allowance for helping out. Alejo would have helped for the fun of it, but he liked the extra money in his pocket and he liked the hotel staff, too. They had started to feel like family, so Alejo tried to do a good job when he talked to the guests. To keep them happy, so they'd ignore the terrible weather and come back to the Pilastro again and again. Still, as Alejo pulled the curtains closed, he couldn't help but frown at the darkening sky. With every room he cleared, his worry grew. Not for himself, because the resort was safe—a fortress on the sea—but for Padrino Nando.

Nando lived in a modest house on the beach next to what had once been a bright pink apartment building. Now it was sun-bleached and crumbling slowly into the sand, along with the rest of La Perla, but Alejo knew it must have been nice when it was first built, when Nando started living there.

Everything was better when it was new.

Before reality set in.

Back then, Alejo's mother had been a little girl and Nando still had hair on his weathered head. It would be years before she grew up and moved to New York City for university and then graduate school, promising her uncle Nando that she'd be back for Alejo as soon as she could make a new start for them. That their lives would be so much better on the mainland, once she had settled into a good career and could stop working two jobs to make rent.

Even that felt like a lifetime ago.

Alejo sometimes heard Padrino Nando worrying about it on the phone with his mother. But he didn't mind. He'd been living with Nando for so long that it felt normal . . . and he was happy in La Perla. He would never tell her—especially not now, when she was so close to making her dreams come true—but Alejo almost dreaded moving to the mainland. He liked sleeping on Nando's faded tweed couch next to the television set, floral curtains blowing in the breeze. The streets always smelled like fried rice and *tostones,* and there was music in the air.

As he busied himself around the resort, Alejo wondered what his *padrino* was doing at home. If he was still watching the skies or if he was reading the newspaper and drinking cold coffee from the morning, a scratchy radio station blaring from the hallway. Alejo scanned the horizon, remembering what Nando had said about the birds . . .

But he didn't see anything.

Just gathering clouds and palm trees whipping in the wind.

La tormenta del siglo—the storm of the century.

Alejo told himself that Padrino Nando would know to return to the hotel if it got really bad. He hoped it wouldn't come to that, but whatever happened . . .

They would be safe at the San Juan Pilastro Resort and Casino.

NEW ORLEANS

JUNE 10—5:00 P.M.

"I'll be back in a bit, okay?" Emily said, more to Elliot's closed door than to her mother, who nodded wordlessly as Emily pulled the heavy apartment door closed behind her. Muffling the television. The afternoon sun filled the hallway, bouncing against the chipped white walls, heating the air like a greenhouse. Emily's arms glistened with sweat as soon as she stepped into the light, but she felt instantly better. She jumped down the scuffed stairs two at a time, toward the noise from the street outside: cars honking, people laughing on their phones, the streetcar rumbling down the avenue.

The sounds of life.

As usual, the front door stuck in its frame, warped by heat and rain.

Emily kicked it open with a *thunk,* then—blinking at the sun—second-guessed herself. She had lived in New Orleans her whole life and still wasn't used to the summers. It was so hot the air shimmered, and she could barely breathe—but anything was better than going back upstairs, to the sadness and the dark.

Emily wiped the sweat from her eyes and jumped down the last remaining stairs.

—

It was cooler once she reached the park, beneath the sprawling canopy of the ancient oaks, but not much cooler. Emily sat on a bench nestled at the base of an especially gnarled old tree, watching squirrels spiral up the trunk into the upper branches. Someone had hung wind chimes from the boughs—enormous, eight-foot-tall tubes—and she peered into the leaves, waiting for a breeze that never came.

It was only when Emily stretched, massaging the crick from her neck, that she noticed the reflection of the sky in the dirty lagoon that anchored the park. It was still and strange, like the world was holding its breath. No clouds danced across the muddy green water, and the feathers that littered its surface floated without movement: curling white castaways from the tiny island where birds nested throughout the year, growing fat off stale bread and minnows.

It had been a long time since Emily had sat in the park like this.

Just thinking.

She was usually on an adventure with Elliot.

Climbing trees or searching for eggs in the reeds by the murky water.

Right before he'd gotten sick, they'd followed the whooping calls of gibbons to the far side of the park, by the river, where a chain-link fence separated the soccer fields from the adjoining zoo. Creeping along the perimeter, they'd peered into empty animal pens until they stumbled across a small hole in the fence by a maintenance shed. Elliot had tried to convince her to sneak in even though they had a membership at the zoo and could have gotten in for free . . . but she'd lost her nerve after he tore his shirt on the rusted wire.

In the distance, a gibbon whooped.

Emily sighed and stared at Elliot's island.

Its trees were ragged with Spanish moss, and even though its banks were only sixty feet from shore, it was easy to overlook the birds if you didn't know what to look for. The trick was to let your eyes adjust to the soft,

dappled light until their feathers and beaks emerged—
like an optical illusion—from the mud and bark. After
that, it was hard *not* to see them: the herons and cattle
egrets perched on low-hanging branches, the shadows
filled with grebes and cormorants and whistling ducks
with tangerine feet.

The little island was so brimming with life that it
seemed to be breathing.

As if it could feel Emily staring, the island exploded
into a low flying arc of gulls and ducks. They circled the
treetops twice before returning to their roosts. As they
settled back down onto the crowded branches, a hot
wind rose, rippling through the lagoon as thick clouds
raced across the sky. Leaves rustled above Emily's head
and the giant wind chimes finally stirred, so quietly that
Emily could barely hear them. She rubbed the goose
bumps from her arms and wondered if Elliot was okay.

If she should run home.

Instead, Emily picked up her book.

"Any good?"

A red-faced woman in neon shorts jogged in place,
checking her pulse. Behind her, a parade of hungry
ducks trailed after a little girl at full waddle. The girl
laughed, waving a piece of bread over her head as her
father jogged to catch up.

"I have two boys about your age."

The woman smiled as she stretched, her ponytail dripping with sweat.

"I just wish I could get them to be more like you— nose in a book, right?"

Emily nodded blankly, but the jogger had already started running again. Her shoes chewed through the narrow dirt path, spitting out tiny clouds of dust as the little girl screeched in her wake. Emily was too old to feed the ducks now, but she rubbed her hand where a goose had bitten her years ago. It hadn't hurt, but Emily had cried because it startled her. As she watched the little girl pushing her way through the scrum of beaks and feathers—laughing, her bread clenched tightly in her fist—Emily decided to be braver.

For Elliot.

There were still a few more hours of light in the day, and she knew exactly what Elliot would want to do if he were with her—but never in a million years would he actually expect *Emily* to do it. Emily hadn't even been able to sneak into the zoo, and this was so much bigger.

She smiled as she stood up and walked to the lagoon's edge.

Looking to see that no one was watching, Emily inched her foot into the water . . . then took a deep breath and stepped in. Her shoes squished into the soft muck at the bottom. She could see the toes of her sneakers just beneath the surface, behind the clouds and her own grinning reflection. Her socks were wet and her shoes felt heavy—but the water wasn't so very deep, and with the haze from the heat, the trees on the little island looked a little like smudges of paint.

Emily slipped her phone from her pocket and held it at arm's length, but she wasn't far enough into the lagoon for photographic proof. To convince Elliot that she'd really walked to the tiny island, she'd take a selfie when she was at least halfway there. And maybe a few pictures from the island itself—looking back at the rest of the park from the muddy banks, with the roosting ducks over her shoulders. Emily laughed as she stepped farther into the water, picturing Elliot checking his messages as she centered her face on the screen.

SAN JUAN, PUERTO RICO

JUNE 10—6:00 P.M.

The lights flickered as wind buffeted the San Juan Pilastro Resort and Casino. The televisions flickered, too, the newscasters fading to black and then crackling back to life midsentence. A reporter with bleached hair and a red blazer said Valerie was on her way to becoming a hurricane and that an evacuation was already under way for the more lower-lying coastal areas. If you lived on the water, she said, it was important to get out. The gusts were faster now—sixty miles an hour over the ocean—and with the wind came waves.

Surges.

The more Alejo watched the televisions, the more he worried about Padrino Nando. While the evening staff bustled back and forth across the marble tiles, preparing for the storm, the news played footage of the beaches on the east side of the island. They were already underwater, for the most part, with whitecapped waves crashing over piers and lapping into the streets. And the worst of Valerie was still over a hundred miles away, they said, churning over the Atlantic.

Picking up speed.

She would hit San Juan sometime during the night or in the early morning, and there was already gridlock on the highway: people driving inland to the mountains, honking through the rain as they inched toward Barranquitas and Orocovis. Alejo watched the broadcasts from an oversized couch across from the revolving glass doors, waiting for his *padrino* to spin into the lobby.

He wouldn't have a choice, if the storm was as bad as they said it would be.

Nando would *have* to come back to the Pilastro.

His house was on the high side of the island . . . technically—but La Perla was nestled outside the city walls and sloping into the sea. Vulnerable. Alejo had tried to call Nando twice from the telephone at the check-in desk, but he wasn't picking up. Alejo chewed his thumb, wondering if he should try to brave the weather and find him. The birds had told them that San Juan would be fine, but Alejo had more information now.

He was only twelve, but even he knew that it was good to get a second opinion.

"*Todos,* everyone!" his manager shouted. "Kitchen, now!"

Despite Alejo's worry and the startling images on the televisions, the atmosphere at the San Juan Pilastro Resort and Casino still seemed celebratory. The last remaining guests were all tucked into their rooms with a hundred reassurances and—even with the flickering lights—everyone smiled as they gathered in the stainless-steel kitchen. The manager smiled, too, winking at Alejo as she announced that there was no need to be scared.

"And why not?" she asked, standing in front of the walk-in refrigerator.

Alejo inched backward, behind the broad shoulders of one of the landscapers.

He knew why *he* wasn't scared: nothing bad could happen to this place. It was too big, and too expensive, but he was smart enough to know that his wasn't the answer the manager was looking for, so he kept his mouth shut and looked at the floor.

"We're not scared—*because we're prepared,*" the manager shouted, throwing open the big silver doors. That was why she had gathered them in the kitchen, to eat the ice cream before it melted. To save them a lot of cleanup tomorrow when the storm had passed, just in case the power went out.

She tossed two pints of vanilla to Alejo.

"Special offer," she said. "One day only."

Alejo accepted the ice cream with a nod, the frost melting on his hands as he squeezed his way out through the growing crowd. *"Sólo los perecederos, por favor,"* the manager shouted behind him. In the rush, some of the staff had started reaching for pillow chocolates and jars of cherries. "Just the perishables!"

He didn't have a spoon, so Alejo tasted the ice cream with a finger as he walked to the empty lobby. It was too sweet for him, and too cold. It made his teeth hurt, but he took another taste anyway as the lights flickered off and on again.

Just to make sure.

In the eerie quiet before the televisions rebooted, Alejo could hear wind howling outside. The loose ends of the ropes they'd used to tie everything down whipped against concrete, slapping wetly without rhythm. The staff laughed and cheered in the kitchen as the manager continued to empty the freezer—but they sounded muffled and distant. It made Alejo suddenly nervous for everyone to be celebrating while Valerie was knocking on their door.

Like they were tempting fate.

Alejo shivered.

Even though they were still talking about the storm, he felt better when the predictions of the newscasters filled the room again—less scared. Less alone. He almost smiled at the commentator with the white-blond hair . . . then frowned when the picture cut away to a reporter in a yellow raincoat.

There was something about the man that Alejo didn't like.

Something that made his stomach drop.

He walked toward the television above the bar for a closer look and felt his mouth go dry. The zigzag tiles of the pool behind the reporter were eerily familiar, and he recognized the stack of blue deck chairs, too. In the background on the television, out of focus—obscured by the rain—was the lobby of the San Pilastro Resort and Casino.

Alejo clutched the two frozen pints of ice cream, his fingers pink with cold.

"Even the most popular tourist destinations are ghost towns now," the reporter shouted. His gelled hair blew stiffly in the wind as he gestured toward the lobby, but Alejo wasn't watching anymore. He was halfway to the revolving door, walking slowly . . . as if the cold marble floor might slip out from under him. When he finally pushed outside, the wall of heat and rain hit him hard, instantly soaking his wrinkled blue shirt.

Squinting against the storm, Alejo scanned the bruised green and yellow sky.

The world outside was different from when he had left it.

The last of the birds were gone, and it was bright—brighter than he expected from watching the footage on the news. Alejo took a deep breath and turned back to the lobby, peering at the televisions through his dripping reflection in the glass doors. He couldn't hear the reporter over the dull roar of the wind and rain, but there he was, his wet shirt clinging to his sparrow's chest in the corner of the screen.

Alejo laughed.

He couldn't help himself.

He turned back toward the cameras, waving the ice cream behind the reporter in case Padrino Nando was somewhere, watching. Beneath him, an emergency alert ran on the bottom of the screen, bright red and flashing. From the mostly abandoned luxury suites of the San Juan Pilastro all the way to Washington, DC, viewers wondered what the boy with the big smile was so happy about. . . .

Valerie was heading right for him.

P7 BETA, GULF OF MEXICO

JUNE 10—6:30 P.M.

"Wake up, Slick."

A man in orange pants and a grease-stained shirt kicked the flimsy legs of a cot as fluorescent lights flickered overhead.

"Ride's here."

The man on the cot groaned as he stretched his arms toward the rivets in the low metal ceiling. Silas "Slick" Thompson had been on the rig for six days already, working twelve-hour shifts on the sweltering deck. When he wasn't working, he was sleeping. That was the job. He didn't see his family for six months out of every year, but the pay was good if you could handle it.

Most people couldn't handle it.

Not all the time, anyway.

Silas had learned that the hard way when his son had gotten sick. He'd been onshore with his family for the diagnosis and for the surgery. That was the important thing. But when it had been time for him to hitch back out to the rig, his wife had grown so quiet he hadn't known what to say.

There wasn't anything he *could* say.

He had to work.

The only promise he'd been able to make was that he'd be home again for the next round of checkups—and that he'd be in touch as much as possible before then. Even if it meant getting teased for video chatting his kids from the crowded galley, he wouldn't disappear into his job again.

He'd be there for them.

"Whaddya mean, ride?" Silas said, kicking off the sheets. He was fully dressed in clean jeans and a white shirt, ready for anything. Anything except a ride back to the mainland. The helicopter wasn't scheduled to pick up his crew for another week. Another week minus five hours, he corrected himself.

He knew exactly when he was going home.

The other man just laughed and kicked the cot again.

"You can wait if you want," he said, stepping into the narrow hallway. "But if it were me, I wouldn't want to ride that chopper in a hurricane."

The oil rig—P7 Beta—was anchored seventy-five miles off the coast of Louisiana, an operation the size of a small city in the middle of the Gulf of Mexico. At any given time, there were over two hundred men and women on the platform. Living together, eating together, and looking out for each other. Silas pulled on a pair of steel-toed boots and followed his friend onto the deck. He was expecting the surf to be choppy, but it was as flat as he'd ever seen it.

Glassy, even.

He shielded his eyes from the sun.

It wouldn't fully set for another hour, but the sky was already blazing with more shades of pink than he could name. A flock of brown pelicans settled onto the mirrored water, wings tucked behind their backs as they floated. Serene. Below him, an industrial supply ship creaked against the rig's huge metal pylons—ready and waiting to carry everyone to safety. A group of roughnecks in yellow hard hats joked with each other as they rode an open-aired lift down to its deck. The shipping forecast had given them an unexpected holiday.

Or an unexpected complication, depending on how you looked at it.

Silas cursed beneath his breath.

The doctors' appointments and the postoperative tests had all been planned around his schedule over a month ago. An evacuation would throw everything off, and if his shifts got shuffled around, his wife would never forgive him.

He'd never forgive himself.

A buzzer sounded as the lift ascended back to the platform, where another group of workers shifted their rucksacks onto their shoulders. Excited for their long ride home. Silas frowned and looked away. There were too many people on the rig to evacuate with helicopters, so they had to take precautions. It made sense, even if it meant shipping most of the crew out early for a phantom storm that might not even hit.

Someone had to run the rig, though.

Someone had to lock it all down if a storm did come through.

If it meant being home when he said he'd be home, Silas figured that someone might as well be him—especially since all signs pointed to a false alarm. From heliport to heliport, it was only a forty-five-minute flight to land. If the waves got choppy, he could always hitch out on a last-minute helicopter. Worst-case scenario, he'd earn some overtime. Even if he didn't, anything was better than a cramped, four-hour float home with the rest of the crew.

Especially if the weather ended up turning.

Then it'd be a rough one.

"Have fun puking," Silas mumbled, waving at the hard hats filing into the ship below. He took one last look at the sea before heading back inside. The sky was about as pretty as he'd ever seen it, and he hoped there was some truth to the old saying about red skies at night being a sailor's delight. Blinking the glare from his eyes, he jogged to find his boss while the gulls laughed overhead, circling the rig in search of the silver fish that gathered there.

NEW ORLEANS

JUNE 10—7:00 P.M.

Emily waded slowly but confidently into the water, angling her phone for a selfie as her feet settled into the thick muck at the bottom of the lagoon. She took short, exploratory steps, trying not to slip while she snapped pictures of her crossing for Elliot . . . but every few feet, the mud gave way to something hard and unyielding.

A rock or a log or a pipe.

She had to concentrate to keep her footing.

Her photos could wait, she finally decided, holding her phone and book high above her head. It was slow going, but the more Emily focused, the more the city seemed to fade into a quiet buzz at the back of her head. Like a gnat, or a fly. *Don't fall,* she whispered under her breath, over and over again, as she inched closer to the tiny island.

Don't . . . fall.

The water was cool—cold, even—but even at its deepest, it barely reached the bottoms of her frayed jean shorts. Algae swirled around her knees and water beetles paddled wildly in her wake. Emily didn't pay them any attention. She just breathed slowly—in and out—as she made her way across the lagoon, wishing her brother could be there to see her.

Lost in thought.

It was only when the wood ducks blinked their orange eyes and dove, disappearing beneath widening ripples, that her concentration broke. By the time their shiny green heads resurfaced, the buzz of the park in the back of Emily's head had grown into a shout. *What if someone sees me?* she thought, her heart pounding in her chest. The asphalt path that looped around the park hugged the banks of the narrow lagoon, close enough that she'd be visible to any passersby—and Emily had never seen anyone in the water before.

It was so dirty that swimming was against the rules.

If anyone bothered to look, she'd stand out like . . .

Like I'm knee-deep in the filthy lagoon.

Halfway to the island with nowhere to hide, Emily splashed quickly to its shore.

The slippery roots knotted into the muddy banks wouldn't have been a problem if she had taken her time. The far side of the island, where field scientists sometimes docked their canoes, had more of a beach, and the island was so small—just two or three times the size of their apartment. If Emily had stopped to think about it, she could have traced the shoreline, stepping onto the sand and out of sight without too much trouble.

She could have played it cool.

Instead, Emily felt as if the entire world were staring at her . . . and one goose, in particular. While Emily scrambled in the slick gray clay, he honked his displeasure as he nipped at her hair. Emily barely had time to scream before she lost her footing and stumbled backward into the muck. As she fell, she threw her book haphazardly to shore. It landed safely in a tangle of reeds—but her phone wasn't so lucky. Emily clutched it to her chest as she paddled through the shallows, panicking as she pulled herself up onto the clay. "Please," she said, wiping a strand of algae from its screen with the hem of her shirt. *"Work."*

She held her breath as she stared into her smudged reflection. . . .

But the screen was dark, and water dribbled from the headphone jack.

Emily sighed as she shook her phone dry.

There was nothing to do but wait.

The island was a rookery, which meant it was full of nests. Emily knew that, but hadn't really understood in her bones what it meant until she'd climbed soddenly ashore, constellations of slimy duckweed clinging to her skin. The birds had scattered at first, feathers literally flying. It wasn't until they returned, shrieking and nipping at her legs and fingers, that Emily realized what she'd gotten herself into.

Soaked from her fall, she found the first tree with a Y-shaped branch that she could reach and climbed it, not stopping until she was sitting as still as possible in the crook of its low-slung limbs. Barely daring to breathe. The trunk was stained white with droppings, and even though Emily was alone on the island—alone and surrounded by a thousand shrieking birds—she could hear her mother sighing as if she were right there with her, frowning at the fresh scratches on Emily's legs and at her soaking wet shorts.

One by one, the birds settled back into the island.

All except for one old Canada goose with a crooked wing. The one that had tried to eat her hair. He was plump from overfeeding, but—hungry for more—he had curled up at the foot of Emily's tree and honked mournfully at her. Ignoring him, Emily squeezed the power button on her phone until it vibrated to life in her dirty hands. Unaware that she'd been holding her breath, she exhaled when the screen glowed brightly with a picture of herself and Elliot before the surgery. As usual, there were no missed calls and no texts. No stars or hearts or likes. Her friends were all busy making new friends at camp and her mom was still on the couch, her hands chapped from overwashing as she watched the news and fretted about Elliot.

Preoccupied.

Propping her phone in the fork of a nearby branch, Emily leaned into the tree and watched the sun start its long descent into the horizon. Pinks and fading yellows streaked the sky, filtering through the Spanish moss on the tiny island. Emily pulled off her shoes and peeled off her socks, curling her pruned toes and smiling. Even though it would be dark soon, she wasn't in a hurry to go home. Not yet. It had taken all her nerve to get to where was and she was determined to enjoy the view for as long as she could.

To remember every minute of it, so she could tell Elliot.

Emily closed her eyes and grinned.

It felt good in the tree. On the island. Away from everything.

She could stay there all night if she wanted to, balanced on the sun-warmed branch next to the family of ducks nestling down into their own feathers. No one could see her from land—not the joggers, anyway. She'd just be a blur to them. And early-morning birders would have to know where to look; Emily had made sure to tuck herself behind the foliage so she was nearly invisible to the outside world.

Like a stowaway.

Hidden from view, Emily daydreamed about running away for real—about making her mother worry about *her* for a change—as she watched a blue heron stalk and swallow a live toad. She raised her phone, zooming in on the toad as it kicked its legs, grappling against the bird's sharp beak until it tired itself out. She swore that she could see it kicking as it slipped down the heron's long neck.

"Gross," she whispered, snapping picture after picture for Elliot.

"Gross, gross, gross."

Sensing her presence, the heron whipped its head toward Emily, its entire body tensing as its yellow eyes locked on her. Like she was next. Emily held the heron's unblinking gaze until it decided to move on, picking its way through the reeds on long black legs without a backward glance in her direction. As soon as she lost sight of it, Emily slouched against her branch, her cheeks flushed from the encounter.

She wouldn't be able to sleep through the night in the tree, she decided.

But it did feel good to be the unpredictable one, for once.

The wild child.

Settling back down into her perch, Emily scrolled through her camera roll and smiled, then checked her messages again out of habit. She still didn't have any, even though it was late enough for a normal mom to start freaking out. She double-checked to make sure that she still had service on the island, that her mother would be able to reach her if she wanted to . . .

But Emily was fully connected—that wasn't the problem.

It would almost be worth it to stay propped in the poop-white branches, she thought, if it would make her mom get up off the couch and notice that she was gone.

Even if it meant spending the night with the heron.

Emily sighed and slipped her phone into her back pocket.

Time moved slowly on the island, so close to home and so far away.

SAN JUAN, PUERTO RICO

JUNE 10—8:00 P.M.

The news crew was still camped out next to the drained pool at the San Juan Pilastro Resort and Casino, huddling beneath tarps and umbrellas as they filmed the rain-whipped reporter. Alejo knew exactly where they were because he had been watching them ever since the cameraman with the scraggly beard had clapped, scolding Alejo for waving in his shot.

"*Oye*, boy," the man had shouted. "No dancing at the funeral!"

The crew had all laughed, yelling at Alejo to get lost. Red-cheeked, Alejo had hidden behind a barrel-chested palmetto, the two melting pints of vanilla ice cream still cold in his hands. After the laughter died down, he'd leaned into the rain, creeping through the cascading bougainvillea to the cabana.

Careful not to get in their way again.

That was hours ago.

Since then, not much had happened.

The paths were littered with leaves—casualties of the wind—and some of the bigger hibiscus had been crushed on the tiles, smeared into pulpy reds and pinks. But most of the flowers were still blooming from their branches. There was no flooding and no felled trees. Not yet, anyway. *La tormenta del siglo* or not, everything was mostly the same as when Alejo had first ventured into the storm.

Only darker.

As a shelter, the cabana wasn't much—just a thatched roof with stacks of scratchy white towels for the pool and cubbies for shoes and purses. But for Alejo, it was perfect. Even without walls, the cabana kept him dry . . . and from its smooth concrete floor, he had an unobstructed view of the camera crew. He wrapped himself in towels and crouched in a narrow crack between the cubbies, making himself as small as possible. Hiding from the wind. Leaning back into the shadows, Alejo smiled as he watched the reporter comb his hair between takes—unaware of the makeup running down his neck staining the collar of his button-down shirt.

"*You* get lost," Alejo whispered.

He didn't like the reporter or the crew very much, not after they had laughed at him. That they were broadcasting live from the San Juan Pilastro Resort and Casino made him like them even less. A small and irrational part of Alejo blamed the news crew for bringing the storm to the island, even though he knew that couldn't be true, and he wished they'd just pile into their rented white vans and drive away.

Still, Alejo watched and waited, hungry for news of La Perla.

So far, the reporter wasn't saying anything he didn't already know.

The wind picked up, blowing rain into the cabana, and Alejo stared longingly at the hotel. From the outside, he thought it looked like it was wrapped in Christmas lights. The Pilastro's windows flickered, golden against the darkness, as the hotel guests followed the news from the safety of their beds.

They may have even seen Alejo, waving in the background.

Before he was shouted out of the frame.

After a while, Alejo's legs started to cramp.

He tried to rearrange himself—to kneel on his knees, at least—but there was only enough room to squat. Through the tall glass windows, he watched his coworkers gather on the lobby's spill-proof couches, eating their way through the refrigerator and following the news. The windows were fogged and it was hard to make out their faces through the rain, but Alejo thought they looked happy. He wanted to join them—to pretend that they were all as prepared as they thought they were—but there was something about the news crew that was keeping him outside in the rain.

Something that made his skin crawl.

He couldn't put his finger on it.

"We're advising everyone to stay off the roads while winds are high," the reporter announced. He said the same thing every fifteen minutes, like clockwork, squinting at his reflection in the camera lens. "A severe wind advisory is in place, and as you can see, there's rain and debris. But as of right now, Valerie is still just a tropical storm. . . ."

Alejo thought he heard disappointment in the reporter's voice.

The reporter *wanted* a hurricane, he realized, his chest pounding with sudden anger.

They all did.

Alejo could tell by the way they joked, their voices too loud with excitement. He could see it in the way the cameraman crept away to the beach between shots, trying to get footage of the biggest waves. For a split second, Alejo thought he might run into the shot again and yell at the reporter. "*You* don't dance at the funeral," he would say, pointing at the reporter and the cameraman and each of the crew members in turn.

Alejo took a deep breath, wondering if he should leave the Pilastro, too—if he should try to reach Padrino Nando before it was too late. A siren sounded in the distance, and then another. They pierced the night, then receded, racing through the storm. *It's still just a tropical storm,* Alejo reminded himself. Too dangerous for him to get back to La Perla, but not dangerous enough for Nando to be in any real trouble.

Not yet, anyway.

Alejo leaned back into the crack between the cubbies, his back flat against the wood. For now, he would stay put, his ears pricked for the sound of the yellow truck rumbling into the parking lot. Nando would never evacuate La Perla, but he would come looking for Alejo. It wouldn't be the first time. If Alejo closed his eyes, he could almost see him turning off the radio and hearing the howling wind outside.

Nando would come running once he realized Alejo never made it home.

That he was stranded at the Pilastro, alone in the storm.

Alejo pulled his cloak of towels tighter, feeling sorry for himself. If Padrino Nando had pulled up in his jan-

gling truck right then, it would have been perfect tim-
ing. Like a movie. But all Alejo heard, for the tenth time
that night, was the reporter shouting his sign-off into the
roaring storm, the black waves crashing in the distance.

"Until then, we're keeping an eye on the skies!"

"Go time," the cameraman with the beard yelled.

"Swells are topping ten feet tall on the east side!"

From his hiding place, Alejo watched the reporter
stalk wetly to the hotel lobby, mumbling about a drink,
while the crew sprang into action. They wiped down
their cameras and coiled their cables at a sprint, running
the packed equipment to the two windowless passenger
vans parked haphazardly on the Pilastro's manicured
lawn. They were so fast that Alejo almost wanted to
warn the reporter. If he wasn't quick about it, he might
miss his ride, and the last thing Alejo needed was for him
to be hanging around the Pilastro all night.

Alejo chewed the inside of his cheek.

As much as he wanted the reporter gone, he enjoyed
feeling like he was one step ahead of Valerie—even if it
meant squatting in the dark cabana in the rain—and he
wasn't sure what to do.

It wasn't just that the news crew wanted a hurricane,
he realized.

It was that they *expected* one.

Alejo's heart beat double time in his chest.

And they were expecting it to be deadly.

By the time Alejo worked up the courage to approach the cameraman who had shouted at him, a lone spotlight was all that remained of the news crew. The bearded man stood beside it, checking the viewfinder of his camera as the rest of the crew waited impatiently in the vans. Alejo shielded his eyes as he walked toward the blinding light, still clutching his melted pints of vanilla ice cream.

"It's the movie star," the bearded man teased without looking up. He showed all his yellow teeth when he smiled, like a wolf. "Back for his sequel."

Alejo shrugged and squinted past the light, the towels draped around his shoulders heavy with rain. Up close, the man's scraggly beard barely covered his hollow cheeks. Like someone who lived in the woods, Alejo thought. He had black Velcro straps hanging all over him. Straps with all sorts of things attached.

"You're a little young to work here," the man said, checking the battery on his video camera. Distracted, he turned away—but Alejo followed him as he strode to the nearest van and threw the rear door open to reveal a bank of monitors, all glowing blue, all playing footage of the storm. *Of the funeral,* Alejo thought, watching the man unload the camera from his shoulder and rifle through a rucksack for a replacement battery.

"My *padrino*'s out there," Alejo finally said. He

pointed down the beach with one of the ice creams. "Do you think he'll be okay?"

The cameraman gave Alejo an appraising look, as if he were seeing him for the first time. His eyes were as yellow as his teeth and Alejo wanted to look away, but he held out one of his melted pints instead.

The man grunted, then accepted it.

"Do you think *we'll* be okay?" Alejo asked.

The man didn't seem to have heard him over the rain.

Instead of an answer, he lifted the cardboard pint to his mouth, drinking the melted vanilla ice cream until it was gone. Before Alejo could repeat his question, the man crushed the container in his hand and tossed it into the empty pool. Alejo flinched. Just that morning, he had skimmed the surface of the pool with Padrino Nando, emptying the fallen leaves and waterlogged bugs into the compost piles behind the kitchen. Even though the sky was already overcast, the water had sparkled when they were finished.

It had been pristine.

"Where's your friend?" the man asked, but he wasn't looking at Alejo anymore.

He was distracted by the footage on the screens.

"La Perla," Alejo said, deciding not to correct him. "By the water."

"We're all by the water," the man said, gesturing

absentmindedly at the resort and the adjoining sea. Just past the tennis courts, the waves that the cameraman thought were too small to film inched slowly up the beach, toward the Pilastro.

When Alejo didn't respond, the cameraman looked at him one last time.

Even in the dark, with his face cast in shadow, Alejo could see his pupils dilate. Adjusting. And for a split second, the cameraman's eyes softened. In that instant, Alejo thought he seemed even older than Padrino Nando. "Sugar rush," the cameraman said, wiping the ice cream from his beard with the back of his arm.

He slid into the front seat of the van and slammed the door.

"My advice?" he said, rolling down the window to clear the fog.

"Stay inside."

NEW ORLEANS

JUNE 10—11:30 P.M.

By the time Emily decided she should probably head home, even the birds were asleep, their beaks tucked beneath their wings for warmth.

Most of them, anyway.

A few whistled and murmured, clucking worriedly into their breasts as a pair of great horned owls hooted in the distance. Emily almost felt like the island itself was quietly fluttering—dreaming—as she scooted down the muddy banks into the murky black water, her phone and book held high above her head. It was easier getting off the island by the light of the heavy yellow moon, with nobody there to watch her except the sleeping birds.

Note to self, Emily thought, splashing into the darkness.

For next time.

The water filling her sneakers felt warmer at night, the air cool on her skin. Sure-footed, Emily waded quickly through the lagoon, her head tilted back to see the constellations overhead. The sky was deeper above the park, away from the lights of the city—it had layers. Grays and purples and blues. Passing clouds cast midnight shadows across Emily's face as the stars twinkled and flashed in the rippling water, lighting her way to shore.

Until she screamed, it was the happiest she had felt in a long time.

Beneath the water, something sharp scraped against her knee, breaking the skin. A waterlogged branch half hidden beneath the lagoon. Emily had been so entranced by the stars that she'd walked straight into it, her legs tangling in the fingers of the submerged limb.

She grabbed it with her free hand, trying not to fall.

"Shoot," she hissed. "Shoot, shoot, shoot."

Three dark shadows splashed from the branch into the lagoon as Emily untangled herself. Turtles, just as startled as she was. *Red-eared sliders.* Only one of them held his ground, barely two feet away from Emily. He stared gloomily into the night while she cursed beneath her breath. As close as he was, Emily wouldn't have been able to see him if it weren't for the moon glancing off his shell. She stood watching the turtle for a long moment, distracted from her throbbing knee.

Somewhere in the darkness, the gibbons howled.

The turtle craned his neck toward the sound, blinking at Emily as if he had just noticed she was there. He twitched, preparing for his great escape, and Emily held her breath. Moving very slowly, she switched her phone and book to her left hand—then pivoted toward the turtle. She thought for sure he would slide into the lagoon before she got to him, but she surprised herself by scooping him up quickly—on instinct, as if she'd been sneaking up on turtles her entire life.

As she wedged the turtle into the crook of her arm, Emily tried to predict what Elliot's reaction would be when she smuggled her new friend into his room. Once he saw what she'd been up to all day—once he was confronted with the scaly, crawling proof—he wouldn't be able to believe his eyes.

Emily smiled as she pictured Elliot laughing.

Clutching his side, in stitches.

But happy.

At first the turtle struggled, scratching her arms with his tiny webbed claws while Emily splashed toward the shore, favoring her right leg. It was only when she reached land that he gave up and retreated into his mossy shell.

"It's okay," she said, hugging him tightly to her chest. "We're gonna be okay."

Safe on land and one turtle richer, Emily inspected her knee.

She was covered in duckweed: little slimy clovers, black against her skin. Beneath them, her legs were scraped and scabbed, old wounds from the morning and before. Emily gritted her teeth, but it wasn't as bad as it felt. The cool air stung, but her knee was barely bleeding. As she stood dripping on the shore, the Canada goose with the funny wing shuffled out of the water, his big brown eyes blinking hopefully. "No," Emily whispered, stumbling backward in her wet shoes. She held the turtle in front of her like a shield, but the goose waddled toward her anyway.

"Go home," she said.

But there was no avoiding him.

The injured goose was so used to being fed and coddled by little children that he acted more like a pet than a wild bird. He rubbed against Emily's bad leg, his feathers soft and warm against the night, then stepped on her foot and honked.

Huh, huh, hunk.

He sounded so mournful that Emily laughed. Now that she was back on the mainland, the park seemed a little more ominous, and it wasn't so bad to have company. Without thinking, Emily reached to pat the goose's head . . . and was surprised when he leaned into her hand. He wasn't purring, she told herself.

She knew birds didn't purr.

But he was *almost* purring.

"You can't come with me," she said. "Not all the way."

The goose didn't respond one way or the other. Instead, he wove between her legs, literally underfoot, as Emily limped beneath the buzzing streetlamps. They were an unlikely trio, she knew, and to top it off, her shoes squeaked. She'd left her socks on the little island, hanging like overripe fruit from a branch of what she now considered to be *her* oak tree. She would have thought it was funny, how loud her shoes were, if it weren't for the rusty creak.

Someone swinging on the old wooden playground.

At midnight.

Who would be here so late? she wondered, her stomach clenching at the thought. She would have run home, but she'd have to pass the swings on her way . . . and with her knee, she wasn't at her fastest. Instead, Emily stopped in her tracks, her ears pricked for danger.

Huh, the goose said, nipping lightly at her ankles.

A white-beaked coot whistled from the lagoon, joining the conversation.

"Shhh," Emily said.

It was nothing she would have thought twice about during the day, but beneath the moon—alone, except for the goose and the turtle—the creaking swing was like something out of a horror movie.

She stayed frozen for one minute, then two.

Long enough for the goose to settle heavily on her feet, roosting for the night.

"It's okay," Emily whispered, more to herself than to her new friends.

Even whispering, her voice felt loud in her ears. Like it was echoing throughout the empty park. The goose didn't seem to mind. He was happily murmuring to himself, already half-asleep, as the streetlights lining the bike path flickered overhead.

Emily peered into the night, waiting for the swing to creak again.

"Hey," someone shouted, and Emily crouched down on top of the sleeping goose. He snuggled against her as she made herself as small as possible, her eyes adjusting to the hazy glow of the streetlamps. The swings were set apart from the rest of the playground and she couldn't see them from where she was hiding, but the red cherries of two cigarettes floated atop the wooden castle by the twisty slide and people were laughing . . . or yelling.

From this far away, it was hard to tell which.

Emily frowned.

Either way, she didn't want anything to do with them.

Her heart beat double time as Emily eased her feet out from beneath the goose and jumped away from the asphalt path. Into the darkness. She felt safer in the grass—invisible, like on the tiny island. *I should have stayed,* she thought as she tiptoed toward the empty avenue, moving slowly to minimize the squeaks.

I could have left in the morning, early.

Before anyone was even awake.

"Everything's going to be okay," Emily whispered, squeezing the turtle's shell tightly against her side. Hugging it for comfort. As she inched her way through the grass toward the well-lit street, it dawned on her that she could only follow the shadows for so long. Beyond the twisted silhouettes of the trees lining the avenue, the city was bathed in an amber light so bright it drowned out the stars.

Once she left the park, she'd be out in the open for anyone to see.

A streetcar rumbled down the avenue, its wheels squealing as it rolled to a stop at an empty red light.

Nobody got off the streetcar and nobody got on.

Still safely in the shadows, Emily took her phone out of her pocket, holding her book over the screen to hide the glow. With a trembling thumb, she found her mom's number and tried to imagine what she would say if Emily called her for help. If she'd yell or if she'd be more quiet-upset, whispering her disappointment as the television blared in the background. Emily's finger hovered over the green *call* button . . .

Waiting.

She stayed like that—waiting—for so long that the turtle peeked his head out of his shell and the goose honked disapprovingly before he fell asleep, nipping at Emily's shoelaces.

She felt like she was going to puke.

It wasn't worth it to wake up her mother, she finally decided.

She took a deep breath and slipped her phone back into her pocket.

They'd have to go home sooner or later.

TROPICAL STORM VALERIE

The little petrel didn't yet realize he was separated from the rest of his flock. He only knew that he had found a pocket in the storm in which to glide, his long legs stretched out behind his white tufted rump. For a sea bird, the petrel was small. And young. It hadn't been so very long since he had been an egg nestled in a rocky islet on the frigid coast of Antarctica. That was where he had fledged and learned to fly, feeding on whatever was careless enough to float beneath his yellow-tipped beak.

That was also where he had been careless enough to cruise right into the scientists' invisible nylon nets. *"Hvad er dit navn?"* the scientist had asked, holding the petrel in the palm of her hands. She was part of a Danish team of ornithologists studying the effects of climate change on migratory birds.

"What's your name, little friend?"

The petrel had stared at her with his tiny black eyes, not daring to move.

The scientist pretended to be offended while she reached for the needle.

Her job was simple: take the petrel's blood as quickly as she could, holding his sharp beak away from her fingers—which were already scratched and pecked by other birds—then cinch a small aluminum band above its webbed foot. The band was stamped with an identifying number and the research team's contact information. Should the bird be caught again, the scientist would know where the wind had blown it.

It had only taken a moment, and then it was done.

The tiny petrel was free to go.

"Det var godt at møde dig!" the scientist had called after him as he wheeled out over the icy Weddell Sea. "It was a pleasure to meet you, my friend!"

That had been almost a year ago, exactly.

Now the band flashed with lightning as the storm swirled around the little bird. He had been flying for days before he had gotten caught in the storm, chasing the deep-sea trawlers that crawled the Atlantic for fish.

Feeding on the snacks they left in their wake.

When the clouds had formed and the sky turned dark, the little petrel hadn't given it a second thought. Storms were nothing to the petrel, who loved flying low above the waves, his long legs grazing the whitecaps as the ocean swelled beneath him. He was small, but he was strong, built for the sea and all it had to offer.

At least, that was what the little petrel thought.

He was too young to know what was coming.

Too young to know that he would be stuck in the eye of the storm, unable to break through the thick walls of wind and rain circling around him. His friends had known—they may have even tried to warn him, but the little petrel hadn't paid them any attention. He'd been too busy darting through the troughs between waves, for the joy of it.

For the thrill.

Now the little petrel flew in the dark, trapped in a pocket of calm at the heart of the storm. He rode the rising currents when he could, trying not to flap. Saving his energy. He was already getting tired, and he was always hungry, but he couldn't stop—not now that he was a part of something bigger than himself.

Not without being battered into the surf.

If he was going to live through this, the little petrel needed to keep flying.

SAN JUAN, PUERTO RICO

JUNE 11—12:30 A.M.

After watching the news vans drive away, Alejo had taken the cameraman's advice and gone back inside the San Juan Pilastro Resort and Casino. He hadn't liked feeling left behind, but he hadn't liked the long-toothed cameraman, either . . . and he didn't have any other options.

Not really.

He could go inside or stay where he was, in the dark.

In the rain.

The lobby had been full when Alejo dripped back inside, so full that that there were no chairs or couches left for him to sit on. He circled the room twice before giving up and sneaking into the cloakroom by the office, where he took off his waterlogged shoes and curled up on the soft velvet settee he knew he would find there.

Beneath the hangers, out of the way.

For a while Alejo had felt happy, surrounded by the muted sounds of people talking and joking and eating the last of the ice cream sandwiches—*just in case*. It was like a party, he thought, nestling into the seams between the cushions. A party where everyone was invited except Valerie. He closed his eyes and pictured Padrino Nando nodding off in his pea-green armchair, the storm raging outside his windows.

Safe.

Alejo was half asleep by the time the hotel manager found him, tucking him in beneath a white feather comforter she'd borrowed from one of the Pilastro's many empty rooms. Ms. Ana knew Alejo well. She knew that he lived with his *padrino* Nando, who helped keep the hotel grounds beautiful. Who arranged a meeting with her every fall, to make sure that Alejo could come to work with him during the summers. The San Juan Pilastro Resort and Casino was a family, so Ms. Ana wasn't worried that Alejo was alone in the cloakroom.

Just that he was wet and tired.

"This rain, it's nothing," she reassured him, pushing his damp hair out of his eyes. "Just a tropical storm."

It was the same line she had asked him to give to the guests earlier in the evening, but Alejo believed her. The comforter was so soft that he felt like he'd been wrapped in a cloud, and as much as he wanted to stay awake and watch the news, his eyelids were too heavy. Nothing bad could happen to them at the Pilastro, he remembered thinking.

Nothing bad *would* happen.

Two hours later, Alejo woke up in a sweat.

The lobby was empty, and as he kicked free from the comforter, unease spread in the pit of his stomach. He had dreamt of cormorants: big, oily black birds racing into the mirrored windows of the resort. Smashing themselves into lifeless bits of blood and feathers. Alejo rubbed the sleep from his eyes and tried to tell himself it was just a dream, that it didn't mean anything . . . but he couldn't help remembering what Padrino Nando had said about the birds.

The birds and the storm.

Alejo shook his head, trying to forget the piercing sea-blue stares of the birds in his dream. It felt wrong, being alone in the Pilastro in the middle of the night. *They wouldn't leave me,* he told himself. But—hidden away in the cloakroom—he was easy to overlook. The rain was beating against the lobby's fogged glass windows in sheets, the roar of the wind so loud he could barely hear the emergency broadcast.

La tormenta del siglo—the storm of the century.

Alejo pushed the comforter to the floor.

The marble tiles were cold on his bare feet, but his sneakers hadn't dried, and the thought of putting them back on while they were still wet was too much to bear. A chill ran through his legs as he padded toward the big screen above the front desk. On the television, a hot pink blob covered the blue of the Atlantic Ocean, trailing yellow and orange over the island. A red band on the bottom of the screen flashed a hurricane warning in capital letters:

¡URGENTE: ALERTA DE HURACÁN, URGENTE!

"Aló," Alejo said, his reedy voice echoing through the empty lobby.

The lights were still on, so he knew it wasn't that bad. Not yet, anyway. But a woman on the television said that the winds had reached over seventy-five miles an hour in the core of the storm, which was heading right toward them. And a high-pitched emergency alert had started screeching at him from every television in the San Juan Pilastro Resort and Casino, like canaries in a coal mine.

Like Valerie, heading right for them.

Where was everyone?

"Hello!" Alejo shouted, jogging to the kitchen.

Half-empty glasses were strewn across the chef's stainless-steel tables, along with the leftovers from earlier. Attracting flies. Alejo shook his head in disbelief. He'd never seen the San Juan Pilastro like this, not *ever.* It wasn't so much that everyone had just . . . disappeared. It was the mess they'd left behind. Alejo frowned, reaching for a crumbling block of cheese. *They wouldn't leave me,* he told himself again, taking nervous bites as he made his way to the breakroom.

From behind the closed door he could hear the television warbling—but when he pushed it open, there was nobody there.

Just empty cookie trays and a half-finished bottle of orange soda.

There was nobody *anywhere.*

Just as he was starting to feel like he was the last person left in the world, the telephone at the front desk began to ring. Alejo ran to answer it, his feet slapping loudly against the floor. "It's Alejandro," he whispered into the phone, in Spanish.

Breathless.

"Where *is* everyone?"

"Hi, yes."

It was a woman with a fancy accent. One of the guests.

The phone felt slippery in Alejo's sweaty hands. "We ordered room service about an hour ago and I was just wondering if that order went through or . . ."

The woman trailed off and Alejo wondered what he should say.

"This is the front desk, right?" the woman asked. "Hello?"

Alejo hung up the phone.

He felt bad about it, but this was no time for room service.

More than anything, he wanted to crawl back into the cloakroom and burrow down, forgetting that any of this was happening. But he knew he couldn't. Not with everyone gone and Padrino Nando out in the storm. Whether he liked it or not, Valerie was coming. Hiding beneath the comforter wasn't going to stop her.

Alejo took a deep breath.

The television said the hurricane was going to hit in the early morning. Predawn, before the sunrise. If he hurried, that was plenty of time to find Nando and bring him back to the Pilastro. All he needed was a ride to La Perla. Alejo kicked himself for listening to the cameraman. He could have been there and back hours ago—when Valerie was still just a tropical storm.

As it was, Ms. Ana had to be *somewhere*.

She would give him a ride, he knew.

Someone would, if he could find them.

If everyone hadn't already evacuated.

"Excuse me, do you work here?"

Alejo jumped.

There was a bald man in the elevator bay wearing an open robe and bright red swim trunks with yellow crabs on them. As happy as his shorts looked, the man looked the opposite. *Crabby,* Alejo thought. Like he wanted to yell at someone. Alejo looked down at his own wrinkled shirt. He wasn't one of the Pilastros' fancy concierges, and he certainly wasn't supposed to be yelled at. He was only supposed to help his *padrino* sweep the bougain-villea petals from the walkways around the pool. To fold the blue and white striped towels, warm from the wash.

"Sorry, mister," Alejo said. *"Quisiera ayudarte, pero..."* *I wish I could help you, but ... not now,* he thought. *Not really.*

Alejo tried to look clueless so the crabby man would assume he didn't speak English and find someone else to bully.

The man's eyes narrowed.

"Aren't you the kid that came to my room earlier?" he asked, his flip-flops slapping the marble floor as he walked toward the front desk. Alejo shrugged as the man rested his arms on the counter. Ignoring Alejo, the man surveyed the lobby. His arms were muscled and hairy. A heavy silver watch hung loosely from his wrist.

"Where is everyone, anyway?"

Alejo opened his mouth to say he didn't know, then closed it as the revolving glass door at the front of the lobby started to spin slowly on its axis. Pushed by the wind. Alejo and the man watched it spit rain and leaves into the lobby until finally, frowning, the man in the funny shorts walked toward the door. He kneeled, clicking the floor lock closed as if he owned the place, and the revolving door stopped spinning.

Outside—in the hot, black night—the storm still raged.

"Excuse me, hi," a woman said, resting two fingers on Alejo's shoulder. He'd been so distracted that he hadn't heard her coming. The man in the crab shorts hadn't either. He was standing stock-still in front of the revolving door, his thick arms limp at his sides.

Watching the storm.

"I just called down about room service and . . ."

Alejo rolled his shoulders, shrinking away from the woman and her thin, cold hands—but again, it didn't matter. She was too distracted by the rattle of the big windows in their metals frames to finish her thought.

"He speaks English just fine," the crabby man said, not looking away from the glass. Somehow, even with the spinning door secured, the rain continued to drip into the lobby. It pooled on the floor, and when the man turned around, his flip-flops squeaked on the wet marble.

"This kid was as smooth as Sinatra earlier. *Everything's gonna be great,* he said."

Alejo didn't like the way the man imitated his voice, high-pitched and singsong, like a cartoon mouse. As the man stared at him, waiting for Alejo to say something—*anything*—one of the deck chairs shuddered across the tiles outside. Unmoored, it bumped into the glass, then slid sideways over the terra-cotta, its wooden feet groaning as it went.

Somewhere in the distance, a siren sounded.

"I didn't realize how bad it was out there," the woman said.

The crabby man just looked at Alejo.

"Where is everyone?"

His voice was hard and cold, but Alejo didn't know.

And he didn't like being left to run the hotel alone, in a hurricane.

It wasn't fair.

"One moment, sir," Alejo said, trying his hardest to sound calm as he looked the crabby man in the eyes. The crabby man smiled crookedly, pleased to have caught Alejo in a lie. It wasn't like he was a genius, Alejo thought.

Just because he was Puerto Rican didn't mean he wasn't American. Everyone on the island spoke English, even Padrino Nando, who spoke mostly Spanish when he had the choice.

The crabby man must have forgotten that.

Or maybe he never knew.

Alejo plastered on a fake smile and backed away from the front desk.

"Let me get my manager," he said without a trace of an accent.

"Told you so," the crabby man said to the lady, turning back to the window. The lady stared at the television over the front desk, pretending not to hear him. Neither of them picked up the phone when it started ringing.

They let it ring and ring and ring.

"That kid's a smooth operator," the crabby man muttered.

As Alejo jogged toward the office, the emergency alert started up again—an urgent, high-pitched squeal. A headache waiting to happen. He knew he'd only find flat soda and leftovers in the back rooms, but it didn't matter. He didn't expect to find the manager, not where he'd already looked. *Manager* was just the magic word—his key out of the lobby. The phone continued to ring as Alejo hurried past the kitchen and the breakroom and into a seldom-used stairwell. Without looking back, Alejo pushed his way through a scuffed metal door and into Hurricane Valerie.

Outside, the rain was harder than he remembered. *Sharper.*

It sliced at Alejo's face and arms, drenching him before he was even halfway out the door. Still barefoot, Alejo shielded his eyes with his skinny arm and splashed through the storm. His plan was simple: circle the Pilastro, checking for lights in the lower windows, looking for anyone who wasn't a guest who might know where everyone had gone. The side door opened onto a path to the pool, so Alejo angled toward the back patio first. From there, he could cut through the parking garage to the front of the hotel.

Bypassing the crabby man and the rest of the guests completely.

Even though the path was sheltered by overhanging balconies, running against the storm was hard work—especially without shoes. The blossoms and petals that had littered the walkways earlier in the day were joined by palm fronds and broken branches, their flesh white and twisted against the black of the night. The wind that had felled them was so strong that it almost knocked Alejo off his feet, so he hugged the walls, creeping like Spider-Man as he tiptoed through the debris.

Trying not to blow away.

It would have been fun ... *if it weren't so terrifying,* Alejo thought, ducking his head against the rain. He braced himself as he rounded a corner onto the back patio of the San Juan Pilastro, stepping into the wind. It groaned as it smashed against the rear-facing wall of the resort, like the cormorants from his dream. Already, the wind had loosened one of the awnings that he and Padrino Nando had secured before the storm, binding them with impossible knots that they expected to cut when the weather had passed. The awning flapped angrily against the cabana, snapping and cracking so wildly that Alejo jumped.

He couldn't help himself.

The thunderous, crashing waves of the Atlantic were close enough that he could feel their spray, but the beach was shrouded in fog so thick that he couldn't see them. Not until the hazy spotlights of the news crew panned across the surf, roiling and gray with foam. Alejo's heart pounded in his chest as towering whitecaps crested angrily toward shore.

The news crew.

And beyond the crew and their spotlights and their cameras ...

A churning darkness.

NEW ORLEANS

JUNE 11—1:00 A.M.

Emily was sound asleep when her phone rang.

She tried to stay that way, ignoring the muffled ringtone—grasping after the last fading tendrils of a half-remembered dream. But it was too late. By the time the call went to voice mail, Emily was more or less awake. She sighed as her phone dinged with a new message, then started ringing again.

Stretching, she opened her eyes.

She wasn't surprised to find herself curled up on the grass, but her mind was still fuzzy. While her phone rang and rang and rang from her pocket, Emily stared up into the dark webbing of branches swaying gently overhead until it all came back to her.

The goose, the island, the turtle.

Elliot.

Everything.

Wind chimes thrummed quietly in a warm breeze, so soft and deep they gave Emily shivers. If the goose hadn't started nipping at her hair again, she might have thought it was all a dream. That she was *still* dreaming. It was only when he stepped heavily onto her stomach that she knew for a fact that she wasn't. *Huh, huh, hunk,* the goose said, his dented beak so close to her face that she almost choked on his breath.

It was awful, like fresh fish and rotting leaves.

"I'm up," Emily coughed, rolling out from beneath her pushy new friend.

Jumping to her feet, she fumbled in her still-wet pockets for her phone. It had to be her mom calling her. If she was being honest with herself, Emily felt relieved. She'd be in trouble—she couldn't imagine *not* being in trouble—but at least she'd be able to sleep in her own bed. The goose stood up, too, his neck stretched tall as he hiccupped his disapproval.

"Stop that," Emily hissed, scanning the darkness for the telltale glow of lit cigarettes.

Remembering.

The park didn't scare her, not really, but the *people* in the park . . . they were still out there somewhere. The swings had stopped creaking, but she could hear them—their voices mixing with the midnight chuckling of restless wood ducks. *And I just let my phone ring about a hundred times,* Emily thought as she tucked her head into her shirt so she could check her messages beneath the damp cotton.

The last thing she wanted was to draw attention to the light.

The second-to-last thing she wanted was to be yelled at, but there was no avoiding that. Emily wondered if her mom would start out worried and then get angry, or if she'd start out angry and go from there. Either way, Emily wouldn't have to wait to find out. As soon as she worked up the confidence to scroll through her missed calls, her phone started vibrating again.

Her hands trembled along with it.

Two calls in a row was bad, but three meant her mom was freaking out.

Like, *about-to-call-the-police* freaking out.

Emily answered quickly, her heart pounding at the back of her throat. . . .

But it wasn't Emily's mom who was trying to reach her.

"Katie?" she whispered, her head still in her shirt.

There was a rustling on the other end of the line,

like a chip bag being crumpled or a phone falling into a lap, but no answer. Just the nonstop reporting of cable news from a distant television. Emily cupped her hand over her free ear, cocooning herself in her wet T-shirt as a hot wind cut through the trees overhead. Upsetting the chimes. "A hurricane warning is in effect," a newscaster said. She heard him as clearly as if she'd been in her own living room, her feet propped on her mom's lap. "For residents living in the red-outlined area, a mandatory evacuation has been ordered. I repeat, a mandatory evacuation has been ordered. . . ."

"Katie," Emily whispered again, as loud as she dared.

Wherever Katie was calling from, it sounded like someone was pulling cabinet doors open and slamming them shut again. There were voices, too—people arguing, *adults*—and Emily strained to hear what they were saying. She was listening so intently that when her friend eventually sighed into the receiver, she almost jumped.

"Em, is that you?"

Emily took a deep breath.

"Hey," she said, trying to sound normal with her head in her shirt.

"Hey," Katie said, bubbling with nervous energy. "This is crazy, right?"

"Yeah," Emily whispered, trying her best to match

Katie's excitement. But she had no idea what her friend was talking about. For a disorienting half-second, she wondered if Katie somehow knew that she was hiding in the park at one in the morning.

"Is, um . . ." Emily trailed off, stumbling as the goose threaded between her legs. "Is everything okay?"

Katie didn't answer right away.

Emily could hear Katie's mom asking her questions from another room, so she listened to the newscasters' banter while she waited. It felt nice, in a weird way, to hang out again—even if it was wordlessly, on the phone. But after one minute passed and then another, Emily wasn't sure if Katie was still on the line. Between the emergency broadcast and Katie's parents, it was hard to make out what was going on. "We're leaving the beach early," Katie finally said, breaking the silence. "Because of the storm and stuff." She barely took a breath between words. "They're saying everyone has to go, so we're getting the car ready now."

Emily popped her head out of her shirt, like a jack-in-the-box.

She was smiling, for the first time since she could remember.

If Katie came home, that would change everything.

"Seriously?"

"Yeah," Katie said, but she sounded distracted.

"Do you . . ." Emily trailed off when Katie's dad interrupted.

He was packing the car and wanted to know if Katie was planning to help.

"Do you want to come over when you get back?"

"We're actually driving up to Atlanta," Katie said offhandedly, like she was used to crossing state lines on midnight road trips. "It's already raining kind of hard here and my parents are trying to leave now so we can beat the traffic. They wanted me to tell you that if you guys end up having to leave the city, you should come stay with us. . . ."

Emily nodded blankly into the night, but of course her friend didn't see that.

In the background, she could hear Katie's mom asking about Elliot.

And Katie's dad hollering from their porch.

"One sec," Katie said, palming her phone.

Emily stared at the matted patch of grass where she'd fallen asleep.

There was no way her mom was going to drive to Georgia—not even if Katie's storm made it all the way to their front door. Not even if her dad came home and thought it was a great idea. Not in this universe. Her mom barely left the apartment as it was, and she certainly wasn't going on any adventures until Elliot was feeling better. Emily sighed and looked for her turtle. The last time she'd seen his angry little face, she'd been cradling him in her arms—and now he was nowhere to be found. She frowned, investigating a clump of clovers with her toe.

He was just a turtle.

He couldn't have gotten far.

Emily paced back and forth across the grass as she listened to Katie's parents clear out of their rented beach house, her eyes peeled for the shine of the moon on a shaggy black shell as the news blared through her telephone. The breeze died out while she walked, and the hum of the wind chimes with it. Katie's television was warning about potential flooding in Florida and Alabama, but it didn't feel like a hurricane was coming—not to New Orleans, anyway. It didn't feel like anything. Katie and her family could drive all night if they felt like it, but all Emily wanted was to find her turtle.

To show Elliot.

"Where *are* you?" she whispered.

She was so focused—so determined—that she didn't notice the group of teenagers huddled beneath a flickering streetlamp until they'd already noticed her.

"Hey," one of them said, more to his friends than to Emily. His voice was deep and ragged from smoking, and his arm cast a shadow so long it felt like it was going to reach out and grab her.

Emily tensed.

But he was just pointing.

She clenched her phone and slowly looked up.

The pointing boy wore cutoff shorts and a faded army jacket, the scraggly beginnings of a beard doing its best to hide the freckles and acne on his cheeks. He and his friends were older than Emily and clearly up to no good. They didn't even try to hide that they were staring at her, their faces bathed in the warm glow of a shared plastic lighter. Emily held her ground as she watched the smoke curling up from the cigarettes in their dirty fingers.

Crawling happily toward them—of course—was her turtle.

Emily took a deep breath and told herself to be brave.

"Hey," Katie said, hopping back onto the line. Her voice sounded too loud in Emily's ear as she walked resolutely toward the teenagers, leaves and sticks crackling underfoot. "I have to go, okay—my parents are already in the car and everything. Stay safe!"

Emily nodded at the boy in the army jacket as she scooped up the turtle with her free hand. "Yeah," she said, using her normal voice instead of a whisper. Straightening her back, she stepped out of the darkness and onto the asphalt—escorted by the goose. He puffed out his chest and flapped his one good wing while the older boys whispered to each other. Emily kept her phone to her ear even after Katie hung up, avoiding eye contact with the boys, who were staring at her like they'd seen a ghost.

"I'll see you soon," she said, pretending she was still on the phone with someone—with *anyone*—to keep the boys from bothering her. The turtle was less shy now and clawed against her arms as she walked past them. Emily clutched him tightly against her chest and held her breath, trying to play it cool—but the goose wasn't having it.

He rushed at the boys, honking and flapping.

Protecting his friend.

"That bird's crazy," one of the boys said.

Emily smiled.

She had been expecting trouble, but the teenagers just cursed appreciatively and stepped back onto the grass. It was only later, when she saw herself in a mirror, that Emily understood why. Her hair was tangled, her legs and arms scratched and caked with mud and algae. She looked like the last survivor of a tropical plane wreck. Like Swamp Thing. Tiptoeing through the midnight shadows with her turtle and the wild goose, Emily had been the bogeyman of Audubon Park.

NATIONAL CLIMATIC RESEARCH CENTER (NCRC)

WASHINGTON, DC

JUNE 11—1:00 A.M.

Joy sucked the last of her soda through the soggy twist of a red licorice straw, then started chewing. Too much sugar made her tongue swell up, but she wouldn't make it to the morning without the rush. Every minute already felt like a lifetime and she was only two hours into her second shift. Yawning, Joy tossed the empty can onto the overflowing bin beneath her desk. It landed with a clink at the top of the pile, then rolled to her feet.

"Only six more hours to go."

Joy rubbed her eyes beneath her glasses and checked the screens.

One of the four monitors was tuned to WeatherTV, which she had muted. The other three were linked up to NCRC-3, a hundred-million-dollar satellite feeding atmospheric data into the NCRC's predictive modeling program. It was state of the art—the heart of their entire operation. The meteorologists at WeatherTV did the best they could with the tools they had, but it was years behind what Joy's team had been able to accomplish with their high-precision technology. NCRC-3 could tell them exactly where a weather system was going, when it was going to be there, and what it was going to do when it got there.

And it wasn't just the reams of data the satellite bounced to their computers every second. It was what they were able to *do* with it. Their Washington office employed no less than ten certified super-brains, all recruited by the United States government. Some were scientists: meteorologists, volcanologists, and geologists. Others were software engineers or sociologists, like Joy. She was an expert in human behavior, which was useful when it came to predicting evacuation patterns and helping cities get their citizens to safety . . . but most of the feeds on the three NCRC-3 monitors didn't mean much to her.

She wasn't a numbers person like the rest of them, and she liked to joke that it was good to have at least one actual human on the team.

Joy reached for another piece of red licorice.

The whole setup was costing a fortune, but nobody ever questioned it.

Not when there were at least ten natural disasters in the United States every year that caused over a billion dollars' worth of damage. *Each.* They happened so often, Joy's team even had a name for them.

BDDs—Billion-Dollar Disasters.

And it wasn't just the money.

Joy wouldn't have worked with the NCRC if that was the case. When a Category 5 hurricane was headed straight for you, it took time for people to evacuate. To prepare. Every minute counted, and the center was able to give people valuable hours.

Days, even.

The NCRC was saving lives, and there wasn't a politician on Earth who would refuse them. They funded the research and development of the NCRC-3 satellite without blinking an eye. And the two satellites that came before it, all of which had the NCRC's motto etched onto their Kevlar hulls.

Forewarned is forearmed.

Luckily for Joy, the system was smart.

Practically smart enough to run itself.

If the NCRC-3 satellite picked up on any atmospheric aberrations, it wouldn't hesitate to let her know. Almost two full days before the last BDD, their entire office had lit up like the Fourth of July. Until the alarms sounded, though, there wasn't much for Joy to do. She wasn't a weather person by training. She was a people person. And right now, when she should have been home in bed, she was the canary in the coal mine.

"Unless the lights start flashing," they had told her, "it can wait for the day shift."

So—ignoring the four screens mounted above her desk—Joy pressed pause on her fifth screen, a laptop she'd propped on her knees. She was four hours into a monster movie marathon and three sodas into the night, and it was time for a bathroom break.

Joy smiled as she made her way through the control center.

Of the ten certified geniuses employed by the National Climatic Research Center, she was the only one who hadn't woken up with a sore throat and a raw pink nose. Which meant she was the best of the best. That was what she was going to tell everyone, anyway. She might be stuck with a double shift, but even the flu was no match for her.

Joy spun an empty chair as she passed it, just because she could.

It was still spinning when her phone started ringing.

She stood in the doorway of the bathroom, waiting for the red emergency lights to activate. . . .

But it wasn't a BDD—it was nothing.

Just a phone ringing in an empty office.

The phone was still ringing when Joy left the bathroom, wiping her wet hands on her jeans. "Okay, hang on," she shouted as she grabbed another soda from the mini-fridge. The lights weren't flashing, but Joy ran to her desk anyway. Her phone was hidden beneath a stack of newspapers, so it took a moment to find it. When she finally uncovered the caller ID, she sighed.

It was Rob.

"Hey," she said, before he could say anything. "Remind me why I'm here if you're not taking the night off?"

"Couldn't sleep." Rob sneezed. "So I was running some of the Valerie numbers and I'm probably not thinking straight, but . . ."

"But what?"

"Joy, my simulations are looking huge."

"Huh," Joy said, scanning the monitors. To her untrained eyes, everything looked more or less normal. Everything except for one blinking number in the corner of the third screen. The most recent number for Valerie's internal speed. It had jumped another fifty miles per hour since the last reading. Rob sniffled as the number turned red before her eyes, setting off a cascading ripple effect across the monitors.

Joy's fourth can of soda slipped to the floor as the

numbers flipped from gray to red, triggering the emergency lights overhead. A Billion-Dollar Disaster. Rob yelled on the other end of the line, but Joy barely heard him as she hung up the phone, immediately dialing another number.

Flu or no flu, this was procedure.

This was why she was here.

"Dr. Carson," Joy said. "I don't want to bother you at home, but you might want to come into the office."

She swallowed hard, her hands shaking from too much caffeine.

"Valerie just turned BDD."

SAN JUAN, PUERTO RICO

JUNE 11—1:15 A.M.

Alejo wiped his eyes with the back of his hand.

It didn't do any good.

The rain was endless. It ran through his hair and down his back in rivulets and rivers that puddled around his bare feet. He even spat rainwater, like it had found a way inside of him.

There was no escaping it.

There was no escaping Valerie.

Still, Alejo stood his ground, squinting through the rain at the familiar glow of the news van. The van was parked haphazardly on a slick strip of boardwalk on the far side of the Pilastro's sprawling deck, across from the hot tubs and the swimming pool. Its windows were lit from within by the soft blue light of monitors and screens, which meant the yellow-eyed cameraman was nearby. Alejo smiled, as relieved as if he'd seen Padrino Nando in the lobby, stirring too much sugar into a midnight coffee.

It was true: the way the cameraman stared through Alejo made the little hairs on the back of his neck stand on end . . . but he'd been out in the storm all night.

He'd been in all kinds of storms.

If anyone could get Alejo back to La Perla, it would be him.

A wet wind whipped around the corner of the Pilastro, chilling Alejo to the bone. He hadn't been lying to the guests when he told them that he'd seen plenty of bad weather. But none like this. None that strangled the beach in fog and blew the skinny palms so hard they almost snapped.

Alejo squared his narrow shoulders and stepped toward the glowing lights.

No matter what, he wouldn't lose them this time.

He couldn't.

Not again.

The path to the beach was littered with twigs and branches, and Alejo half regretted leaving his shoes to dry in the cloakroom—but there wasn't time to go back. He picked his way toward the van quickly, without a second thought. It was only when lightning flashed across the sky that he slowed. *Horror-struck*. In the split second before the thunder, he could see everything as if it were frozen in time: the awning, pulled taut—like a sail— and tangled in a power line, its thin metal cables lashing wildly in the wind, just steps away from Alejo.

When the thunder finally cracked, it was so loud that Alejo shook.

The dirt beneath his feet was soft with rain, the mud warm between his toes.

He sank into it—stunned—as the metal cables snapped against the cabana, hard enough that Alejo swore he heard the wooden posts splinter and then split. He'd been heading toward the cabana out of habit. If the lightning hadn't struck, if he hadn't seen the power line . . .

Alejo took a deep breath and peered through the darkness.

The billowing fabric of the awning was lit from below by the cabana's television. Its screen flashed red, casting the awning in a soft pink light. From where he was standing, Alejo could just barely hear the newscasters. Valerie's winds had topped a hundred miles an hour, they said, their voices half lost in the rain. And she was still gathering steam over the Atlantic. By the time she reached the island, she'd be even stronger.

"Catastrophic," they said.

Alejo strained to hear more, but couldn't.

Not over the creak of the cabana as the awning struggled to free itself.

It twisted tortuously in the wind, slowly ripping the power line from its mooring. Metal brackets wrenched loose and rusted nails fell to the ground as the power line sparked. Alejo clapped his hands over his ears, bracing for an explosion.

As if on cue, the television went dark and the sky opened up with lightning.

If Alejo had looked up, he would have seen huge banks of gray clouds racing overhead—Valerie's outstretched fingers, reaching ominously toward land. There wasn't a bird in sight. They were long gone, but Alejo was too distracted to notice. Finally free from the cabana, the awning soared over the empty pool like a parasail, its cables trailing calmly behind it. Frozen in a sickly white flash of lightning, it looked almost alive. He blinked the water from his eyes, wondering how far inland the awning would fly, but by the time the thunder clapped again, it had fallen back to earth, the power line limp and lifeless in its wake.

Alejo held his breath, waiting for fireworks.

But there were no sparks and no flames.

Just a low, rumbling thunder and unrelenting rain.

The piercing wail of sirens cut through the night, and

in the distance, the lights of the camera crew continued to shine. Crouching low against the wind, Alejo gave the downed power line a wide and careful berth as he made a break for the pool. It felt so strange, that it was empty. Even in the off-season, the pool was warm to the touch and postcard blue. Dazzling with reflected sunshine. Alejo helped skim its surface with a long net every few hours to keep it that way.

"These people only *visit* paradise," Padrino Nando would say, gesturing at the recliners as he emptied his net into the trash. "How lucky for us to live here!"

Lucky, Alejo thought, gripping the rattling aluminum ladder so tightly his knuckles whitened. He hated to see the pool drained. Dirty water puddled in the deep ends, and with the sirens warbling overhead, it felt like he was climbing into a bomb shelter. But despite everything, Alejo felt some of Padrino Nando's luck as he hopped the last few feet to the concrete floor. The tiled walls shielded him from the worst of the storm, and even with Valerie raging overhead, it was quieter beneath the water line.

Calmer.

Alejo trailed his fingers across the blue and white tiles as he jogged through the basin of the pool, toward the news vans and the breaking surf. The pool snaked around the cabana like a lazy river, and his bare feet splashed against the smooth cement as he followed its curves—sprinting beneath arched footbridges and banking around the tall concrete walls of manicured islands. Alejo didn't slow down until he was in the shallows, the wind ripping through his hair at full force again.

Red-faced, he squatted to catch his breath.

He was close enough to see the bleached white teeth of the reporter from where he was sitting, but he couldn't hear him. Not over the wind and the crashing waves. The fog was so thick that Alejo could still only see the ocean in fragments: windswept and jagged swells, tall enough to dwarf the vans, crashed angrily into their own shadows, spitting sea foam into the rippling wind.

Alejo's chest tightened with panic.

The reporter was a big man—tall and broad-shouldered, perfect for the evening news—but he looked like a little boy next to the mountainous sea. One strong gust, Alejo thought, and he'd be in the riptide.

Never to be seen again.

The hair on Alejo's arms stood on end as he watched the sea gnash its teeth at the shoreline. It wasn't until the news crew moved in for another shot that he realized he wasn't alone. Huddled behind one of the vans, staring open-mouthed into the encroaching waves, was Ms. Ana—drawn to a scene she'd recognized, with horror, from the lobby's many televisions. She looked small and scared. Like a child. If she hadn't been flanked by one of the chefs and the night concierge, Alejo would have thought she had lost her parents.

"*¡Aló!*" he yelled, waving his arms.

The concierge clutched his stomach and frowned, then vomited behind the van.

Even if Ms. Ana and the chef hadn't turned to comfort the concierge, none of them would have heard Alejo. It was too loud, so close to the sea. Alejo swallowed the sour splash rising at the back of his throat, then spat. Every instinct told him to run back to the hotel—to stay inside, to stay safe. Like the last remaining guests of the San Juan Pilastro Resort and Casino—two dozen stranded tourists, secure in their rooms. Or the rest of the staff, who had disappeared while Alejo was sleeping, either to abandoned hotel suites or home to their families.

Away from the worst of the wind and the rain.

But Alejo couldn't go back to the Pilastro.

Everyone he loved was out in the storm.

There was nothing to do but join them.

Rainwater oozed through the cracks in the boards as Alejo stepped onto the boardwalk. He took one step and then another, his toes spreading on the slick wood as he tested his weight. The boardwalk shifted beneath his feet, turning his legs to jelly. "Severe damage is expected on the north coast of the island," the reporter shouted into his microphone. "If you live in any of these areas, a mandatory evacuation is now in place."

The cameraman had his video camera trained on the reporter, but his eyes were locked on the black, webbed waves behind his back. They were so close that Alejo could have reached out and run his fingers through their troughs. Too close, he realized. His stomach dropped as it finally hit him. The beach was gone, the entire sandy crescent swallowed by the surf.

And the boardwalk rocking beneath his bare feet felt like it would be next to go.

Alejo's heart pounded as he ran to join the hotel manager by the vans.

"Ms. Ana," he yelled, but she didn't turn to look at him. He tugged on her sodden sleeve. When she finally tore her attention away from the waves, she blinked at Alejo as if she were waking from a dream.

"Ms. Ana, we need to get out of here."

"Alejo!" she shouted into the wind. Her was voice was raw, like she'd been yelling all night. "What are you doing here?"

"What are *you* doing out here?"

"We saw him," she said, pointing at the reporter. "On the news."

The night concierge nodded weakly, then ran to the back of the van to be sick again. "I need to go to La Perla," Alejo said, trying to keep his voice from breaking. "I need to go home." He didn't mean to sound so upset, but the glistening eye of the video camera had started circling him, drawn to the drama of the moment. Alejo could feel it taking everything in and could only imagine how he would look in the morning papers, soaked and shoeless.

He didn't like it.

"*Oye,* movie star," the cameraman shouted from behind his camera, his lens still trained on Alejo. "I thought you were in for the night?"

Alejo shrugged, squinting angrily at the camera.

"You gotta wait until morning to go anywhere," the cameraman said. Alejo could hear the years of tobacco in his raspy voice but couldn't see his face. Just his scraggly beard peeking out from behind the camera. In the big black lens, Alejo watched the corners of his own mouth twitch into a frown. "It's a state of emergency in La Perla. Mandatory evacuation," the cameraman shouted. "National Guard's there and everything."

Ms. Ana squeezed Alejo's shoulder, but he rolled out from beneath her grip. Freeing himself again. He didn't want to cry, not in front of the video camera or Ms. Ana, but he could feel his face crumpling as she walked over

to the cameraman and whispered in his ear. The cameraman nodded, and Ms. Ana ushered Alejo to front door
of the idling van. There was no way she was going to let
him walk back alone—not now that the storm was reaching a fever pitch. He would ride back to the lobby with
the rest of them instead, once the news crew had finished filming.

"It's okay," Ms. Ana said, rubbing Alejo's back as she
opened the door.

The heat was already on and there was a towel draped
across the passenger seat.

"We know you're worried. We're all worried, but
everything's going to be okay, *verdad?*" She waited for
Alejo to nod, then smiled with tight lips and slammed the
door closed. Alejo sighed, pointing all the heater vents at
his face. He shivered for a moment, on the verge of tears,
but felt less hopeless as he warmed up and took stock
of the van. It was mostly empty. There were no monitors and no expensive equipment. The backseats were
strewn with wet plastic ponchos and backpacks waterproofed in trash bags.

The other van was the control center, he realized.

Alejo's van was just the extra.

The rain drummed on the windshield and Alejo settled into the towel.

Everything's going to be okay.

Ms. Ana was so nice that he almost believed her.

Almost.

Alejo reached next to the steering wheel and turned on the wipers, his hand grazing the keys in the ignition. Even with the wipers on, it was hard to see. They weren't fast enough to keep up with the rain. Nothing was. The beach was already gone, and high tide was in a few hours. It would take the boardwalk with it—and there was no telling what else it would take.

If Alejo wanted to find his *padrino,* he couldn't wait until morning.

Not if it was a state of emergency in La Perla.

Everything's going to be okay, Alejo told himself, crawling into the driver's seat.

The keys jangled across his knees as he stretched to reach the pedals. Wishing he'd paid better attention when Nando worked them in his yellow truck.

It wasn't so hard.

Nobody even noticed the big white van inching off the boardwalk, its revving engine masked by the raging winds. They were too focused on the rabid sea and the rising waves. As he bounced over the lawn—stretching to reach the gas and tap the brakes—Alejo caught a glimpse of the San Juan Pilastro Resort and Casino in the rearview mirror. The windows looked golden against the night.

Warm.

It made it harder for Alejo to drive away.

To leave everything behind.

But actually *driving*, on the other hand, was easier than he expected.

Like riding a roller coaster without the tracks.

PART TWO

FLEDGING

fledge (verb): to acquire feathers large enough
for flight

—*Oxford English Dictionary*

P7 BETA, GULF OF MEXICO

JUNE 11—1:30 A.M.

There were exactly twelve crew members remaining, down from the usual two hundred fifty—enough to fill up an emergency helicopter, if it came to that. They spread out on well-worn couches in the common room, shifting uneasily in their seats. Not paying much attention to the shoot-'em-up playing in the corner. The movie was easy to ignore. They'd all seen it a hundred times, and the volume was so low it was practically a whisper. Quiet enough that Silas could make out the gentle lull of the ocean against the steel pylons beneath them.

When the storm rolled in, they wanted to be able to hear it.

If it rolled in.

There was a good bet going about whether or not it would even rain.

Silas and the rest of the skeleton crew had taken that bet when they decided to wait Valerie out on the rig. The rest of the crew—the ones who evacuated—had put money on it. They'd already been home for hours. Silas had gotten texts from some of them: selfies in their trucks, showing off thick hamburgers and fries in the parking lots of their favorite restaurants. Holding up twenty-dollar bills. "I got three times this much says you're gonna be stuck there for a week," his rig-mate wrote. "Livin' on oatmeal and wishing you'd listened."

Silas ignored their texts.

He was too tired to joke around.

They all were.

They'd worked late by floodlight—the last remaining twelve—securing the enormous platform as best they could. They'd tied the cranes down into their cradles and cleared decks the length of two football fields. It was heavy work, and every so often Silas had wiped his brow and stared into the horizon, wondering if the reports could possibly be true.

Silas shifted in his chair, then stood—making his way out of the breakroom and onto the deck. He still wasn't sure what to believe, and now that their work was finally done, his mind wouldn't stop racing.

He needed some air.

He needed some reassurance that he hadn't messed up.

The moon was set low in the sky, reflecting brightly against the placid Gulf. When Silas looked at it long enough, he saw layers and layers of stars in the distance. Whole galaxies he'd never seen before, strewn like shattered glass in the purple depths beyond the Milky Way.

But no hurricane.

Silas pushed his sleeves up his sweaty arms and told himself he'd made the right decision. It had taken them a full six hours to prepare for the storm, and in all that time, he hadn't even felt the *hint* of a breeze. The weather people had gotten everything wrong, as usual. There was nothing left to do but lean over the rusted railing and watch the seagulls gather in the gentle swells. The operations manager joined him, spitting wetly into the wavelets.

"You know how much it costs to shut this thing down?" he asked, not waiting for an answer. He wiped the spittle from his lips with the back of his arm. "Eight hundred thousand dollars. Per day, not counting lost revenue."

The operations manager shook his head and stalked away with a pained expression on his face, like it hurt him personally to have to send everyone home and lose all that money. The truth was he didn't have a choice.

It was procedure. Lost lives were more important than lost revenue. But on the rig, revenue meant oil, which is what they were all there for in the first place, so of course they waited until the last possible minute to shut off the valves.

When the operations manager finally pressed the button, Silas thought he'd feel the entire platform shudder to a stop beneath his feet—but nothing happened. The manager looked like he was going to have a heart attack, but there were no other signs that the rig had turned into a billion-dollar lump in the middle of nowhere, with no land in sight.

Silas shook his head as he made his way back to the common room.

"All this for nothing," he said, settling onto a weathered brown couch. "I don't think it's even coming." The other eleven could have gone back to their bedrooms. They could have gone anywhere on the rig: the gym, the galley—there was even an actual theater—but they all stayed with Silas in the common room, not saying anything. Half-watching an old action movie they'd all seen before.

Waiting for the sound of rain on steel.

When it finally came, it was like fat fingers tapping on a hollow wall. So slow you could almost hear each individual drop. Silas cocked his head as the operations manager took out his phone to make a call. Just as he walked out of the room, the tapping fingers formed a fist—the rain pounding against the offshore rig so hard it shook. The eleven remaining workers sat listening to the storm as Silas paused the movie, trying to gauge how big it was as the waves pounded against the pylons, echoing up into the drum of the empty rig.

Reverberating.

"Just got word from the mainland," the operations manager said as he blew back into the room, his clothes so wet they clung to his arms and legs. He was breathless from his phone call and looked almost relieved. "It's actually happening. Waves are fifteen feet tall and growing. Good thing we evacuated, right?"

The rig creaked in the sudden wind and rain.

"*We* didn't evacuate," Silas said. "Not us. Not yet."

He wasn't sure if he should call his wife.

He didn't want to scare her, but it looked like he was coming home early after all.

SAN JUAN, PUERTO RICO

JUNE 11—2:00 A.M.

Alejo hunched over the wheel of the borrowed van, peering into the darkness.

He had tried to find the headlights as he splashed through the storm, but after twisting and pushing every knob on the dashboard, he'd only managed to turn on the radio. It glowed with the signal of a satellite floating twenty-two thousand miles above Australia . . . but the lights were still a mystery to him.

It hardly mattered.

He hadn't seen another car since he'd left the Pilastro, and the fog was so dense it was like swimming through milk.

The rain only made it worse.

Alejo bobbed his feet on the pedals—gas and then brake and then gas again—as he veered off the empty road into the heart of the city. The asphalt gave way to cobblestones and the steering wheel vibrated beneath his fingers. On any normal night in Old San Juan, he would have seen couples lingering in secret alleys, glowing from a night of dancing and cocktails, and men puffing cigars while feral cats stalked between their legs—all in the soft amber light of gas lamps, with live music from open-air restaurants mingling in a warm sea breeze.

Salsa and jazz and marimba, a different song for every block.

Tonight, there were no cats and no couples.

No men smoking cigars.

Even worse, it was as if they'd never been there in the first place. The windows of the storefronts and restaurants lining the plazas were either shuttered or boarded up with fresh planks of wood. Alejo drove slowly, looking for signs of light and life. But the cracks between the colorful plaster and the plywood were dark. It was a complete blackout.

A ghost town.

He had never seen the city so empty.

With everyone gone, the narrow streets felt almost spacious, as if they'd expanded to fill the void. It made Alejo feel lonely, like he was driving through a cemetery.

He rubbed the chill from his arms as the rain picked up, battering against the windows so loudly it drowned out the hum of the engine. Stepping on the gas, Alejo nosed the van toward La Perla with wide eyes. He made it less than a block before the windshield fogged up for the hundredth time.

"Come *on*," Alejo muttered, stretching to wipe the glass with the tips of two fingers. The clear smudge fogged over almost immediately, but not before he saw a metal trash can jump the curb in front of the van, spilling paper plates and wet napkins as it tumbled across the street.

Alejo stomped on the brake, his heart pounding. . . .

But even with the pedal pushed all the way to the floor, the van didn't stop.

Not entirely.

Alejo's stomach clenched as the rear wheels fishtailed behind him, skidding on wet cobblestones until the van was finally caught in the arms of a fruiting calabash tree.

No airbags deployed.

No alarms sounded.

And there was nobody to run to the scene of the accident to see if Alejo was hurt. Outside the fogged windows, it continued to rain as if nothing had happened. Alejo cursed, quietly at first and then so loudly it would have drawn attention . . . if there had been anyone in Old

San Juan to hear him. His breath was rapid and shallow as he turned in his seat to survey the damage. A hairline fracture ran through one of the rear windows and the roof buckled under the weight of a low-hanging branch.

But he was fine.

Everything was fine.

The adrenaline receded as quickly as it had come.

Alejo slumped behind the wheel and turned the radio off, his foot still on the brake. It wasn't a regular plastic trash can. That would have *actually* been fine. This one belonged to the city, one of the heavy steel cans planted on every other corner—indestructible by design. Alejo's breath caught in his throat as he rubbed the shivers from his arms. He could still hear it crashing down the empty street, chipping away at the cobblestones and curbs.

Picking up speed.

The cameraman was right; it was too dangerous to be out.

But there was no turning back now.

The roof of the van popped back into place as Alejo tapped the gas, the branches of the twisted tree clawing against the paint and steel. He cringed at the sound of it, at the squeals and the scratches. The cameraman wouldn't like the damage, but there was nothing Alejo could do about that. His only choice was to keep moving. He was so close to Padrino Nando's little house. He just needed to follow the curve of the street toward the sound of the breaking surf.

And to watch out for trash cans.

Alejo rolled the windows down and let the wind and rain in.

It was the only way he could see the road.

Just ahead of him was Castillo San Cristóbal, the old Spanish fort next to La Perla. Alejo had played there a thousand times, running in its courtyards and hiding in its tunnels. There was a legend that the spirits of the sea gathered at its crumbling walls. They said you could hear them whispering on darker nights. That some of the soldiers who stood guard at the turret closest to the waves had even disappeared, never to be seen again.

La Garita del Diablo, they called it.

The Devil's Turret.

Alejo hadn't believed the stories, but there was a weathered plaque to commemorate the soldiers who had lost their lives. He'd seen it with his own eyes. Padrino Nando had made a point of showing him. As Alejo drove toward San Cristóbal with the wind in his hair, he couldn't help but think of his *padrino* and the Devil's Turret. The night was dark, and even from a distance, he imagined he could hear the spirits whispering.

In fact, they were practically screaming.

He turned the radio up and flipped through the stations, drowning the *diablos* out while traffic lights swung precariously overhead. Creaking on their cables. Alejo turned the radio up even louder—as loud as it would go—as he navigated the heavy van down the last short stretch of road before Padrino Nando's house. Calle Norzagaray. The narrow street ran along the top of the old city wall, overlooking the Atlantic—separating Old San Juan from the sea.

La Perla was on the wrong side of the wall.

Neither city nor sea, it sat perched on the sloping beach between the two.

Despite the ocean views, no tourists went to La Perla.

Nobody went to La Perla unless they lived there, not even the police.

That was the saying, anyway, and it was true—La Perla wasn't in any of the glossy travel brochures they kept behind the front desk at the San Pilastro. But for Alejo, it was home. It hadn't always been easy, but he'd been happy to live there with his *padrino* ever since his mother had left for the States. And until she was able to make a life for them up north, La Perla was the only home he had.

Alejo stepped on the gas.

The roads to La Perla were meandering. They skirted the water, looping back and forth across the length of the beach before feeding down to the shore. Alejo had often driven these roads with Padrino Nando, who cranked the windows down in his rusted yellow truck to take in the sea breeze. To catch up with friends and neighbors. Even without the small talk, the roads were the slowest way down to their little yellow house.

The fastest way into La Perla was by foot.

Alejo pulled off Calle Norzagaray, bumping over the curb onto the grass of a small park. The song on the radio crackled as it spiraled into a falsetto chorus, the heavy rhythms mixing with the crashing waves as Alejo drove down a short sidewalk that was well worn by his own footsteps. Set into the top of the ancient wall, unmarked except for a few hasty graffiti tags, was the entrance to a set of concrete stairs. Alejo put the van in park just in front of the stairs, on the precipice of the wall, and waited for the song to finish.

Hesitating.

All the lights in La Perla were out—the first victims of the storm—but he could hear Valerie's waves slamming against the beach just a few hundred feet away. He rubbed his hands in front of the heater vents, gathering his strength. There was no predicting what he would find at the bottom of the stairs once he made his way down to the sea, and with wind moaning and the water rising, it was harder than he thought it would be to open the door and walk into the storm.

I'll be quick, Alejo told himself, remembering the sparkling lights of the San Juan Pilastro. For a long moment, he wished he were back in the cloakroom, curled up on soft velvet settee beneath a fluffy white comforter. Once he found Nando, they'd go back. They had to. Everyone would be worried sick about them—and even if they knew it was Alejo who took the van, Ms. Ana would understand.

It was a state of emergency.

They hadn't given him a choice.

Just as Alejo was about to run into the rain, he remembered the ponchos and stopped himself. Crawling to the second row of seats, Alejo pulled one of the clear plastic ponchos over his head, then ripped open the waterproof garbage bags, digging into the backpacks inside. Taking stock. He found mostly dry clothes, dry socks. Dry shoes. A few books and some chargers. Alejo held the shoes up to his own bare feet, but they were all too big. There was nothing he could use—and besides, he was going home.

Climbing back into the front seat, Alejo opened the glove compartment.

He rifled through it, looking for a flashlight.

Instead, he found a small black phone. It was heavy-duty, with orange rubber reinforcements. Not a phone, Alejo realized. A walkie-talkie. Just one, which meant that somebody, somewhere, had its mate. Alejo pressed the trigger and held his breath—but all he heard was static.

He decided to take it anyway.

Just in case.

As soon as Alejo pushed the door open, the rain filled the van, carried by the wind. He struggled to slam the door shut again, then ran across the top of the wall without bothering to lock it. His poncho fanned out behind him in gusts so strong he thought he might fly off into the sea, so he scuttled on his bottom, sliding through the grass and the mud to the relative safety of the sheltered stairs. He slipped down the first few in a panic, then rested against a cracked cement wall—finally in La Perla.

Alejo exhaled, spitting rain from his lips.

The houses were built so close together, and the stairways so serpentine, that the wind broke before it reached him. A small silver lining on a hundred black clouds. He cleared the water from his ears with his pinkies and popped his jaw. The sirens were louder than at the San Juan Pilastro. Their rusted speakers—built into the parapets of the old wall—modulated high, then low, piercing through the din of the crashing surf.

Warning Alejo of the danger he was heading straight into.

Alejo could tell from the sound of the waves—from the *closeness* of them—that the beach was flooded, like at the Pilastro. Unlike the Pilastro, the beach was narrow in La Perla. On a good day, high tides swept tangled seaweed halfway to the houses that were closest to the waves. And on a bad day? Valerie had helped double the reach of the sea. The lower houses were already flooded with salt water and sand, their inhabitants long gone. Driven to the rural inland mountains, to Barranquitas and Orocovis.

Escorted to safety by the National Guard.

A mandatory evacuation.

Alejo prayed that his *padrino* hadn't been among them—that he wasn't truly alone in the storm—but he could feel the panic rising in his chest as he pulled the wet hood of his poncho tightly around his head. There was no way of knowing until he checked, so he clutched the walkie-talkie in a trembling fist as he made his way down the rest of the stairs to the little house he had grown to love. Most of the windows he passed were tacked shut with warped wood, repurposed from shipping crates and skateboard ramps. But in some of the windows, through the slats of closed shutters, Alejo could see the warm flicker of candles, and as the sirens faded out and then in again, he heard muffled voices behind closed doors.

Voices and music, even.

Neighbors.

Like Alejo, they refused to be scared off.

Rain streamed down Alejo's face as he grinned into the night. It ran into the neck of his poncho and worked its way back down to the ground, soaking him from head to toe. Alejo didn't mind. *He wasn't totally alone.* Padrino Nando's yellow truck was still parked on the asphalt in front of his matching yellow house, and Alejo rapped its hood with his knuckles before jumping the last few feet onto the porch.

"Nando!" he shouted.

He tried knocking twice, then a third time, his smile fading when nobody came to the door. He would have peeked through the window, but the shutters were all firmly closed, so—finally—he turned the knob. It wasn't locked. The door opened noiselessly into Padrino Nando's house, which was twice as black as the night outside. Alejo stumbled blindly into the living room, shrouded in darkness.

"Anyone home?"

He felt his way around the couch and the coffee table, his knees knocking into chairs and corners as his bare feet slapped wetly against the wooden floors. "It's me, Alejo," he called out, his voice cracking as he felt his way through the empty rooms. It didn't take long. Padrino Nando's house was neat but small. There was a bathroom and a kitchen, a bedroom—and the futon where Alejo slept, beneath the windows overlooking the sea.

Alejo sat on his futon, in the dark, cradling the walkie-talkie in his lap as the wind whistled and moaned overhead. La Perla was slipping into the waves and the National Guard had swept through the streets of Old San Juan until it was a lifeless shadow of itself . . . but Alejo had heard his neighbors eating and drinking and waiting out the storm. He hadn't imagined that—he'd seen the lights through their shutters with his own eyes.

Not everyone had evacuated.

But Padrino Nando was nowhere to be found.

NEW ORLEANS

JUNE 11—7:30 A.M.

Emily rolled in bed, kicking the sheets from her dirty legs.

The air in her room felt stale, the pillow flat and hot beneath her cheeks. Outside her bedroom door, she could hear her mother talking in low and serious tones. As always, the television was blaring. It chimed with another breaking update as Emily wiped the drool from her chin with the back of her wrist. "He's not home yet," her mother murmured, pacing toward Emily's door and then turning back to the living room. "But he'll be okay—they shut the rig down last night, just to be safe."

Emily groaned, reaching for her phone.

It was seven-thirty in the morning.

She closed her eyes and did the math.

She'd only been in bed for five hours and the sun was already so bright that she could see it through her eyelids. There was no way she was getting back to sleep, so—awake and exhausted—Emily thumbed through her feeds instead, looking for signs of the storm that was cutting Katie's beach vacation short. She wasn't sure what to expect, but everything seemed normal. Except for Katie—whose wide orthodontic smile was missing in action—her friends were all sharing pictures of their super-fun summers: selfies in front of sparkling lakes and late-afternoon ice cream cones.

Emily thought about posting the pictures she'd taken from her perch on the tiny island, but even with her favorite filters, they were too weird and murky. She barely recognized her own face beneath her tangled hair and she was out of focus in every shot, so she sent them to Elliot instead, grinning with expectation as she waited for his reply.

Chewing her lip as seconds turned into minutes.

And minutes stretched to fill the morning.

When her battery symbol flashed red, Emily let her phone slip into the folds of her sheets and sighed. The rest of the apartment still smelled like lemon and vinegar, but Emily's room had grown thick with clutter—notebooks and magazines and stuffed animals floating

on mounds of unwashed laundry. Her charger was somewhere beneath the mess, and she wished she'd had the
heart to find it the night before.

After her midnight escape from Audubon Park.

Looking back on it from the safety of her sunlit bed,
Emily felt almost invincible.

Her goose had refused to follow her when she'd crept
out past the trees. . . . He'd flapped his good wing in
protest, honking as she jogged beneath the streetlights.
Making a ruckus. Waking up the neighborhood. But by
some miracle, Emily had managed to sneak her turtle all
the way home without getting grounded for life. She'd
eased the door open and shut it quietly behind her, kicking off her muddy shoes before climbing the stairs.

Tiptoeing past her mother, who'd been curled up on
the couch.

As usual.

It had taken the last of her energy to change into a
wrinkled pair of old pajamas and toss her still-wet clothes
beneath her desk. Expertly filling the last clear spot on
the floor. "Ten points to Gryffindor," she'd mumbled,
collapsing back onto her pillows, her eyes heavy with
sleep. At some point in the night, her turtle had crawled
beneath the damp pile—drawn by the familiar scent of
duckweed. He stayed there through morning—his head
and tail hidden from view, unmoving until Emily stirred.

As she stretched awake, he slowly emerged from his shell, his eyes wide as he tracked the dust motes floating through the soft morning light. The air was thick with them, and the turtle snapped back into his shell as Emily sneezed into the crook of her elbow.

She sneezed again, and again, her face red and crumpled from the effort.

As she rubbed her nose with the hem of her pajamas, the footsteps in the hallway stopped, then slowly turned back again. The weather forecast spilled into her room as her mother knocked twice on the door, then opened it without waiting for an answer. "One second, Lil," she said, muffling the receiver as she peeked at Emily from the shadows.

"You're not getting sick, are you?"

From the hallway, her phone voice had sounded normal.

Happy, even.

But as her mother stood in Emily's doorframe, her face looked drawn and pale. Like she'd been crying. Her red-rimmed eyes locked on Emily as if Emily had the plague and her nose flared at a smell she couldn't quite place. "You can't be around Elliot if you're sick," she said matter-of-factly. "You know that, right?"

Emily stared at her mom from beneath knitted brows. She didn't know what to say.

It was like her mother had forgotten their shared nights in the hospital, falling asleep on hard plastic seats. Eating stale pretzels from the vending machine and trying not to lose hope. Emily wasn't stupid. She'd been in the room when the doctor sat them down and explained how their lives would change when they brought Elliot home. How everything would be fine, *if* . . . The doctor had listed everything they needed to do—all the precautions they had to take—while her mom quietly sobbed with exhaustion and relief.

Everything's going to be fine, Emily had whispered.

Squeezing her mother's small, cold hands.

Everything's going to be fine.

Emily remembered all of it, every aching minute.

But she didn't say any of that.

Instead, she tried as hard as she could not to roll her eyes.

"I'm *not* around Elliot," she said, her words cutting through the morning like broken glass. Sharp and jagged. "I'm barely allowed to see him." She wished it hadn't come out that way, so confrontational, but it wasn't fair. They were supposed to be in this together, Emily and her mom—not turning on each other while they wasted their summer in front of the television, spraying so much Lysol they could taste it at the back of their throats. Not hiding from the world as if their bodies had given up on them, too.

As if they'd given up on themselves.

Her mother flinched, then hardened.

"Emily," she said. "He's not out of the woods yet. His immune system . . ."

Emily shook her head.

"I know," she said, swallowing the second round of sneezes she felt itching at the back of her throat. She held her breath as she watched small particles of dust swirl in the light between them, but her mother didn't say anything. She just scowled at Emily from the doorway, the phone pressed tightly against her chest.

"I *know*, okay," Emily repeated, sounding calmer than she felt. "I'm not sick. It's just"—she gestured at the mess—"I need to clean my room, is all."

Her mother frowned, then nodded, wrinkling her nose at Emily's wet clothes. The turtle crawled out from beneath her desk as if on cue. *No,* Emily whispered to herself. *Not now.* But her turtle didn't listen. His square little head peeked out into the sunshine as her mother checked the corners of the ceiling for traces of mildew. "Make sure you get beneath the bed," she said, stepping into the hall. "Something's . . . *gross* in here." The turtle's upturned nose mirrored her mother's almost exactly, and Emily's lips twitched into an unexpected smile as her mom put the phone back to her ear and stepped into the hallway.

She was lucky her room was so messy.

If it had been any cleaner, her mother would have seen the turtle. A sneeze was one thing, but a wild animal from Audubon Park was something else entirely.

One look at his mossy shell and she would have short-circuited.

"Sorry about that, Lil," her mom said, shaking her head as she walked away.

As soon as the door closed behind her, Emily sneezed again . . . and again. She fell back onto her pillows while the turtle clawed its way toward a pair of tangled earbuds. It felt good to sneeze, and Emily stretched herself awake for the second time that morning as her turtle gnawed contentedly on the knotted cords. She watched him for a full minute, mesmerized by his determination, before she started patting her sheets—searching for her dying phone.

"Glamor shot," she said, zooming in on her turtle's crossed eyes.

She snapped five quick pictures, then chose the best one and traced a pink heart around his scaly head so he wouldn't blend into the detritus of her room. Grinning at her handiwork, Emily texted the photo to her brother. *Are you awake yet?* she asked, her charge slipping from ten to eight percent. While she waited, she checked her messages . . . but she still didn't have any. Not from Elliot and not from Katie and not from any of her other friends. Except for Elliot, who was sleeping fifteen feet away, they were all out living their own lives.

Having fun, like regular kids.

Or evacuating, like Katie.

Cramped in the backseat of an overpacked Toyota, driving north out of Florida.

Even that didn't sound so bad to Emily, considering the alternative: two more months alone in her dirty room, bored out of her mind with no one to talk to and nothing to do except finish her summer reading. She picked at the dirt beneath her nails, glancing around the room for her mom's old copy of *My Side of the Mountain*. It wasn't on her bookshelf or stacked on top of her dresser with her other books. Unless it had somehow settled into a secondary layer of laundry on her floor, Emily wasn't sure where it could be. The turtle stopped chewing on her earbuds and blinked at Emily, jogging her memory.

Shoot.

She jumped out of bed, rifling through the clothes on the floor for a fresh pair of shorts and a clean T-shirt.

Even though she needed one, she didn't have time for a shower. She'd left her book in the park. She remembered it now. Not on the island, but on the grass, where she'd fallen asleep. It was so old it was probably worth something—another reason for her mom to be mad at her. The turtle watched Emily with curiosity, ducking back into his shell as she picked him up and stuffed him without warning into the big pocket of her empty backpack. Just beyond her bedroom door, her mom shuffled back and forth in the darkened hallway, finishing her call. "Honestly, I understand why you'd worry, but the weather's totally fine here," she said, laughing politely. "It's better if we don't move him around too much."

Hovering.

"Okay, then," her mom said. "We'll just wait and see."

As soon as she hung up on Aunt Lillian, she threw Emily's door open again.

Emily stood in the middle of her room, dirty but dressed, her backpack at her feet.

"Good," her mom said. "You're up."

Now that she was done pretending to be happy on the phone, her voice was back to normal. The mask of a smile was gone—changed in an instant to the expressionless thin lips Emily had grown to recognize. She held out a handful of bills, crumpled from her purse, and set them on Emily's overflowing dresser. "This is for pizza or something," she said. "I need you to stay with Katie for a day or two, just in case you're coming down with something."

A chill ran up Emily's arms despite the heat.

She was almost too stunned to argue.

"Isn't there a storm coming?" she asked.

Emily's mom slumped against the doorframe, looking almost like her old self again as the television played two cat food commercials in a row. Emily could feel the turtle rearranging himself in her backpack while kittens meowed onscreen. "We'll figure that out when your dad gets home," she said. "But a little rain is nothing compared to what we've been through already."

Her face tightened, and Emily nodded.

It was easier not to fight when her mom was like this.

There was no winning—and she was just worried, Emily knew. She was worried and she was tired and she was alone. They both were. Emily slipped her phone into her back pocket and slung her backpack over one shoulder. Her mom had made up her mind, and there was no point in telling her that Katie wasn't around.

That she didn't have anywhere to go.

Not really.

Emily closed her eyes and wished for her dad to walk through the door right then. She wished as hard as she could, but when she opened her eyes, nothing had changed. "Elliot can't handle a cold right now," her mom said, her voice even and calm. Like everything was normal. It was hard to look at her without crying, but Emily looked up anyway—squinting through tears.

Her mom looked tired, like she was the one who was in recovery.

She looked *sorry*.

"We just can't risk it," her mom said. "I'll call Katie's parents; they'll understand."

She forced a smile as she waved Emily out of her own room.

"It'll be fun, okay?"

"Okay," Emily mumbled, trying to keep her voice flat and steady as she took the bills from her dresser. She folded them into her pocket slowly, taking stock of her bedroom. It was hard to know what to pack when she didn't know what she was doing or where she was going, so she decided not to bring anything at all.

Just her turtle in her backpack and a pocketful of cash.

She'd be back soon enough, anyway.

It was only a matter of time before her mom found out that Katie and her family were in Atlanta. As soon as she got around to calling them, she'd panic and call Emily. She'd tell her how sorry she was for sending her away and beg her to come back home. Even so, Emily wasn't happy about it. She wanted to sprint past her mom and into Elliot's room. To give him a hug and tell him everything she'd done. To show him her turtle. But instead she walked through the sunless living room, past the cold glow of the television and into the foyer, her stomach growling as she pulled her mud-encrusted shoes onto her bare feet.

Her shoes were still wet, and they squeaked as she plodded down the stairs.

But Emily was too angry to cry, and too hungry to be angry.

Pushing the front door open with her shoulder, she stepped into the morning light, squinting as she smoothed and counted the crumpled bills on the sun-dappled steps. It didn't take long—she had one twenty, two tens, and three one-dollar bills. Forty-three dollars in all. A strawberry milk was a dollar and nineteen cents at Winn-Dixie, and they sold doughnuts there, too. Big, sticky ones—the glaze so thick it pooled in hard white piles at the bottom of their wax paper wrappers.

Emily could almost taste them just thinking about it.

She swallowed.

She was on her own, and her lost book could wait.

It was a long walk from her apartment to the grocery store, but Emily knew where she was going. She just had to follow the traffic away from the park and not stop until she reached a series of sprawling parking lots. Fields of black asphalt baking in the sun. She stared at her shoes as she walked, kicking rocks beneath the flowering crepe myrtles. Halfway to the grocery store, she realized she was humming tunelessly to herself and looked up. Squirrels chased each other across fresh-cut lawns and entire families rode their bikes toward the park, laughing as they dodged potholes and off-leash dogs.

It was another beautiful day in New Orleans.

Emily sighed.

Her arms were turning pink from the sun, and by the time she reached the grocery store, she felt more guilty than angry.

It wasn't always easy, but she loved her family.

If anything happened to any of them, she didn't know what she would do. . . .

An old minivan honked—two beeps, short and insistent—as she stepped onto the blacktop. The parking lot was as packed as she'd ever seen it, and Emily had to weave through gridlock to reach the entrance. Somewhere behind her, someone shouted out their unrolled window and the honking escalated. As it reached a crescendo, Emily looked for her friend—the security guard who always smiled—but he wasn't in his usual spot. His cracked plastic chair sat between the entrance and the exit, empty except for a folded newspaper and a half-finished booklet of word searches. A young woman pushed past her as she stood in front of the sliding glass doors—her purse knocking into Emily, *hard,* as she hustled into the air-conditioning. The woman didn't stop to apologize, and Emily rubbed her shoulder as she followed her into the store and out of the sunshine. After her eyes adjusted to the flickering fluorescent lights, Emily noticed the security guard pacing by the registers.

She waved, but he was too distracted to notice her.

She didn't blame him.

The grocery store was a madhouse.

Emily usually lingered by the candy and comic books stocked at the front of the store, but the checkout lines were so long that they snaked in front of her favorite displays. It figured: now that she had money for *Batgirl* and sour straws, she couldn't get to them. Everywhere she looked, carts were filling the aisles, piled high with bags of bread and bottles of water and boxes of cereal—entire shelves pushed into baskets, like the store was going out of business.

Like there wasn't going to be anything left for her.

Emily half jogged through the frozen food aisles, juking past slow-moving shoppers and spinning around abandoned carts. There was less traffic at the back of the store, and less food on the shelves. Emily's stomach clenched as she reached the bakery—preparing itself for the worst as she slowed, walking past the empty shelves in disbelief. There weren't any glazed doughnuts or chocolate-covered doughnuts or jelly doughnuts— and there wasn't anything else, either. Not even a burnt apple turnover or a stale baguette. The entire bakery was cleaned out except for a dented white box that had been kicked halfway beneath a rolling wooden island.

Emily kneeled onto the scuffed tiles and inspected the box.

It was a cherry pie, crumbled from its fall, with dark red syrup oozing through the broken crust.

Emily didn't care that it was a floor pie.

It was perfect.

She cradled the box protectively against her chest as she jogged back to the front of the store—stopping just once, to grab one of the flavored milks the security guard seemed to like so much. There was a cow in a berry patch on the label. The cow was licking its lips and giving Emily a thumbs-up. She smiled to herself as she found her place at the back of the checkout line, three carts behind the woman who had knocked into her outside. She wouldn't have recognized the woman's face, but she remembered the faded pink of her oversized purse. Emily stared at the back of the woman's head as the rest of the store eddied anxiously around her.

There was a buzz in the air—an excitement that bordered on aggression.

If she hadn't been so hungry, Emily would have left her crumbling pie on a shelf and walked right out the smudged glass doors. But she'd skipped dinner the night before and her stomach churned, loud enough to remind her that she'd been kicked out of her own house before she'd had a chance to eat breakfast. Not that there was anything good in her kitchen, anyway—just off-brand Cheerios and hard green apples. . . .

But Emily wasn't sure when she'd be back, and she was *hungry*.

So she stood patiently, waiting for the elderly cashier to ring up the overloaded carts in front of her. The line hadn't moved one inch by the time the security guard noticed her—the one person in line with five items or less. "You here with your momma?" he asked, waving as he ambled toward the back of the line. Emily shook her head, and the guard carried her pie and strawberry milk as he guided her toward the front of the checkout line, placing it on the belt as the woman with the pink purse scowled at her from behind her cell phone.

Emily didn't pay her any attention.

"Customer emergency," the security guard said, his voice loud enough for everyone to hear as he winked at the old man working the checkout. "This is my buddy," he whispered. The old man smiled at Emily, handing her a plastic spork from beneath the register as she unfolded her money. "You got the right idea," he said, chuckling as the security guard resumed his patrol. "Girl after my own heart."

Emily smiled back at him and slipped the change into her pocket.

The sun reflected off the hoods of the cars in the parking lot as she stepped into the heat, tempting her to sit in the security guard's empty chair. In the shade. Emily perched on the edge of his seat, not wanting to disturb his newspaper. The picture splashed across the front page was an aerial shot of the flooding in San Juan. The roofs of the houses looked like islands in the surf. DESTRUCTION AT DAWN, the headline read, the black ink smeared where the guard had folded the page in half.

Emily drank her milk first, watching the cars circle the lot for spaces that didn't exist. There were no clouds in the sky, but it wasn't blue. It was more of a yellow-ish green, like plastic left out in the sun. A weird color, to match her day. Emily wiped the pink froth from her lips and started in on the pie. It was so sweet it gave her a headache, but she didn't care. She had already eaten her way through the better part of it when her phone vibrated in her pocket.

A text from Elliot.

Finally.

Mom's crying again, he'd written, leaving off the period.

Letting the observation hang in the hot summer air.

Sorry, Emily texted, her screen sticky with syrup from the cherries. All of a sudden, sitting on the security guard's cracked plastic chair in front of the crowded Winn-Dixie, Emily felt like crying too.

"Did you really bring a turtle home?" Elliot texted.

A tear fell on Emily's screen, blurring his message.

She had five percent battery left and had forgotten her charger in her room.

SAN JUAN, PUERTO RICO

JUNE 11—8:00 A.M.

Alejo blinked awake in the dark to the sound of whistling, tuneless and high-pitched. Like a teakettle boiling over. He kicked his legs off the futon and onto the cold wooden floor, reaching beneath the frame for his spare pair of sneakers. The power was still off and the shutters were pulled tight, so there was no telling what time it was or how long he'd slept. The only thing he was sure of was that the storm was still raging.

He could hear it, just outside the door.

Waiting to get in.

"Aló," he called out, his voice echoing through the empty house. "Is anyone home?"

Except for the knocking of the wind against the shutters, there was no answer. He was lucky the shutters had held through the night. That Padrino Nando had made time to lock his house down against the storm. Others hadn't, and the squalls blowing in from the Atlantic had only gotten stronger while Alejo slept. They'd broken most of the windows in La Perla in the small hours of the morning and had been whipping across the cracked and jagged glass ever since.

Moaning as if they were bleeding.

As if they were alive.

Safe inside—cocooned in darkness—Alejo tried his best to ignore the wind. He stumbled to the old-fashioned armoire and pulled what he needed from the hangers. He was sore, his bony shoulders aching from the tense drive home, but it felt good to be wearing a fresh shirt and a dry pair of shoes.

He blindly knotted his laces, then rubbed the crust from his eyes.

Alejo had hoped he would wake up to a new day—a day without Valerie. That Nando would be brewing coffee and boiling eggs as he stretched in bed, the sunlight hot on his sheets. Like nothing was wrong.

Like usual.

But he was still alone.

And Hurricane Valerie was far from over.

Alejo opened the front door, shielding his eyes.

It wasn't that it was bright out, but it wasn't dark either. It was somewhere in between. Somewhere Alejo had never seen before. He squinted, casting a long shadow in the empty house as he blinked the sky into focus. The rain had let up for the time being, but the horizon in all directions was a wall of gray, unbroken except for a thin green line splintering between the gathering clouds. The wind swept roughly across the waves, spitting seawater onto Alejo's clean clothes and whistling so loudly he covered his ears.

But he didn't run back inside, to where it was dry and safe.

Not even as the ocean spray stung his eyes.

Instead, he gripped the doorway, steadying his legs, and took in what was left of La Perla. He was even luckier than he had realized. The storm surge had reached the asphalt in front of the house while he slept. Any farther and he might not have made it to morning. Alejo watched the waves lick the tires of Padrino Nando's truck. It had flipped overnight, capsized by the rising tides, and its windows had collapsed under thick piles of sand. The sand filled the entire front cab, leaking out of the cracks in the door like a broken hourglass. Everything beyond the truck—the honeycomb of brightly colored houses, stitched together with power lines and tiled mosaics. The empty pool where the skateboarders spent sunburned afternoons, flying up the curved walls into the cloudless sky. The crumbling stairway down to the beach, overgrown with crawling vines and banana plants . . .

It was all gone.

Swallowed by the steel-gray sea.

The front door swung on its hinges, tapping Alejo's back as the waves slapped against their newfound shore. He was so lost in thought that he almost didn't notice the woman waving to him from the stairs beside their house. "Hey," she yelled, straining to be heard above the white noise of the wind. Her hair was tied back in a thick ponytail and an overstuffed laundry bag was slung over her shoulder. She was with two men who were also carrying bags—garbage bags, packed to bursting. They kept climbing the stairs as the woman shouted at Alejo, their broad shoulders bent against the wind.

"¡*Oye*, boy!" the woman yelled. "You can't stay here!"

Alejo stared blankly at the woman and her friends.

She was right, he knew—but he was too stunned to move.

His pulse quickened as Padrino Nando's ruined truck groaned beneath the weight of wet sand. He wanted to run with every fiber of his being, to leave before it was too late. But Alejo stood frozen on the porch instead, his legs numb with shock as the woman stood steadfastly against the wind, waving for him to join her.

"*¡Vamos!*" she shouted. "Everyone else, they're already gone!"

But Alejo couldn't leave.

And he couldn't stay, either.

Not with La Perla sinking beneath the waves. The truck would be the next to go, and then the house. And then Alejo, if he didn't get moving. But wherever Padrino Nando was, it felt wrong to leave without him. The woman yelled at Alejo again as he ran back into the house, the door slamming shut behind him. "We're out of time," she shouted, cursing loudly as he disappeared inside. "We can't wait any longer!"

Alejo barely heard her.

He was too busy unlatching the shutters and throwing open the windows, letting what was left of the sun into the house he shared with Padrino Nando. A day-old newspaper fluttered on the dining room table and the curtains billowed in the salty breeze as Alejo jogged from room to room, rifling through the old man's belongings in the strange yellow light.

Looking for a sign.

A clue.

Anything.

But everything was in its place.

Nando's summer blazer hung from a hook behind the kitchen door, and his wooden pocketknife and pipe were resting on his bedside table, worn smooth from decades of use. Padrino Nando wouldn't have left without them.

He wouldn't have left without *Alejo*.

Not if he could help it.

Alejo slipped the knife into his pocket.

He ran his thumb across its handle as he swept through the rest of the house twice, and then a third time for good luck. The heft of it was reassuring in his hand, like a part of his *padrino* was still with him, protecting him. But the truth was that he had left a long time ago, like Alejo should have.

It wasn't until he worked up a sweat that Alejo admitted it to himself.

Padrino Nando was gone.

A sudden gust of wind ripped through the open windows, knocking a framed photo from the wall. The glass shattered, the shards exploding across the hardwood floor. Alejo could have closed the windows and looked for a broom, but he sat heavily at the kitchen table instead, resting his forehead on the cool white tiles.

Closing his eyes.

La Perla was drowning and his *padrino* had left him and there was nothing Alejo could do about it. He had tried his best . . . and there was nothing he could do about any of it. *"Dame fuerza,"* he whispered, clenching his fingers into a fist.

Give me strength.

But Alejo didn't even know where to start.

Sighing, he slouched into the stiff-backed chair.

It was only when he rubbed the tears from his eyes with the back of his hand that he saw the note. It was folded into a small square and wrapped in a plastic sandwich bag that was duct-taped to the table so it wouldn't fly away. Alejo sat up in his chair and scraped the tape from the tile with his thumbnail. Even with the note still folded in plastic, he could make out his name through the back of it. Padrino Nando had pushed down hard with a blue ballpoint pen. . . .

So hard the paper had ripped.

Alejo's heart pounded as he unsealed the bag.

As he unfolded the note and started to read, the woman with the thick ponytail climbed into the driver's seat of the van she had found at the top of the wall—its keys in the ignition, like a sign from God. She crossed her heart and told herself that the National Guard was still patrolling. She'd call them as she drove—she'd flag them down if she had to. She'd do whatever it took to make sure the boy made it out alive. But she wouldn't stay in harm's way any longer, not with the worst of the storm breathing down their necks. *She couldn't.* Two other families were already piled in the backseats, their entire lives packed in overflowing trash bags on their laps.

Waterproofed, like the old man's note.

The last of La Perla.

Alejo squared his shoulders and squinted through the windows of Padrino Nando's house, at the darkening horizon, as the van scraped over the sidewalk and onto Calle Norzagaray. The wind continued to shriek and sirens sounded throughout the city, but he'd grown accustomed to the noise. It was the oncoming clouds that bothered him. He refolded the note and stowed it in his pocket as he studied the sky.

There were layers to the haze that he hadn't noticed before.

There was movement.

The corners of Alejo's mouth twitched downward as stacks of clouds blurred into focus. It wasn't just haze that was making the sky gray. It was the massive inner wall of Hurricane Valerie, a centrifuge spinning at over a hundred miles per hour, tracing a deadly circle around the island. The bright green veins flashing through the cracks in the clouds: lightning trapped within the depths of the storm, flickering like a dying bulb.

Alejo stepped outside, craning his neck as he searched for a break in the wall.

A break that didn't exist.

The wind swept his hair back from his forehead and thunder echoed over the Atlantic. Alejo fingered the note in his pocket as the rain picked up again, cascading in sheets across the last remaining bits of La Perla. Washing the hot tears from his face. The note was short and had been written in haste. *"Lo siento,"* it read in a tightly slanted cursive. "I'm so sorry, Alejo. I tried to stay for you, but I didn't have a choice. Call your *mami* as soon as you can, and remember," Padrino Nando had written. "The birds . . ."

They always come back.

NCRC

"This can't be right."

Clusters of pixelated storm fronts spiraled across the bank of monitors above Joy's desk, converging on the southern seaboard. Their coverage was so dense that Joy's boss—Abigail Carson, PhD, director of the National Climatic Research Center—was having trouble making out the red outlines of the map beneath them.

"Is that . . . ?"

She squinted at the map, but all she could see were shades of gray.

"Florida, Texas, Alabama, Mississippi. Everything Joy said.

Their latest numbers had Hurricane Valerie makir

153

landfall in T minus 12 hours. Even if she'd been a normal hurricane, it would have been a national emergency, but Valerie wasn't a normal hurricane.

Not by the time she reached the Gulf Coast.

Not by a long shot.

That was thanks to a trio of low-pressure systems currently brewing in the Caribbean Sea. On their own, they were just bad weather: board games at the hotel instead of swimming at the beach. If it wasn't for Valerie, they'd be blips on the NCRC's scanners. Now they were all anyone could think about. As Valerie passed over Cuba and the Dominican Republic, the low-pressure systems would be swept into her widening vortex. The cable news channels were already calling it *the big one.*

Joy was trained to deal with Billion-Dollar Disasters— they all were—but Valerie's projections made her skin crawl. She was too big, the size of three hurricanes rolled into one . . . and she was moving too fast. Faster than any hurricane they'd ever tracked before. Throttling at full speed toward the coast and spanning hundreds of miles, she'd be completely unstoppable.

Joy raised a paper cup of vending machine coffee to her lips, then set it down without drinking it. She'd been up for over twenty-four hours and was so full of soda that her blood was practically carbonated. As good as the coffee smelled, if she had any more caffeine, there

was a chance she'd never sleep again. Instead, Joy closed her eyes and settled into her chair. Valerie was only getting stronger, but the flashing red lights had long been disabled and the alarms quieted, replaced by a chorus of blowing noses.

Flu or no flu, all hands were on deck.

They'd been on deck since Joy sounded the alarm at one in the morning.

The whole team had been coughing and sniffling and draining cup after cup of burnt coffee to shake off their nighttime cold medicine—but they were at their desks, preparing for the coming storm. Joy took a deep, meditative breath and tried not to think about germs while Dr. Carson studied the monitors.

"Rob," Dr. Carson said, her voice barely a whisper. "Run these numbers again, okay?"

Rob rubbed the raw, red wings of his nose with the back of his wrist.

He'd been parsing NCRC-3's satellite feed for seven hours without a break, tweaking his algorithms. Trying to find the best-case scenario he hoped was hiding somewhere in the reams of data, like a needle in a haystack. "I've checked nine times now," he said. "Every time, she's on track to go mega."

Dr. Carson thumbed through the contacts on her cell phone as she strode purposefully toward the hallway.

Stepping out of the control room, she looked up to lock eyes with Rob. "Run it a tenth time," she said. "And hope we got something wrong."

Rob shook his head.

The numbers never lied, but there was no arguing with the boss.

He would have tried to, but she was already gone.

Joy watched Rob clack away at his keyboard, his eyes reflecting the blue glow of the computer screen as he worked his magic. Even with disaster looming, Rob smiled as he updated his projections with the most recent readings. Like everyone Joy worked with, he lived for the big stuff: earthquakes off the Richter scale, tidal waves the size of skyscrapers. His thrill was in the numbers—the bigger, the better—but Joy was paid to think about the people on the other end of his equations. The people who were going to meet Valerie, up close and personal, whether they wanted to or not.

Through the glass door, Joy watched Dr. Carson pacing as she talked on the phone. One of her hands was thrust into her pants pocket while she punched the air for emphasis. The walls were reinforced, so Joy couldn't hear what she was saying, but even from a distance she could see Dr. Carson's face reddening as she shouted into her cell phone, clutching it so tightly Joy wouldn't have been surprised if it shattered. As tired as Joy was, she felt a sudden, unexpected relief at not being on the other end of the line.

She took a tentative sip of her coffee, then drained the entire cup.

There was no chance she was going home. Not anytime soon.

"Huh," Rob whispered.

Joy turned to see a smile corkscrewing across his chapped lips. "What is it?" she asked, leaning forward in her chair, but the red lights started flashing again before she had the chance to walk over and see for herself. "What happened?" she shouted, raising her voice to be heard above the emergency alert and the two desk phones that had started ringing at the same time. Rob was so entranced by his numbers that he barely seemed to notice.

The numbers didn't lie—he was right about that much. . . .

But they could change.

The phones clicked over to voice mail, then immediately started ringing again—but still, nobody answered. Fresh data streamed across the monitors, scrolling so quickly it was impossible to read. Even just glancing at the screens, Joy could tell it was bad. The numbers were more red than black, and red wasn't good—it was easy enough to interpret. Past that, Joy would need a doctorate in atmospheric science to know what exactly the numbers meant. She held her breath as Rob's program finished loading, then studied the swirling visualization of the storm that filled the monitors. It was the same mass of gray smothering the same map of the southern United States.

Except for the projected landfall, it seemed unchanged.

It took Joy a moment to isolate the difference.

When she did, she felt as if she'd had the wind knocked out of her.

Where the bold readout in the top corner of the screen had once predicted T minus 12 hours until landfall, it now flashed T minus 10 hours. To lose two hours of traveling time, Valerie would have to be traveling at incredible speeds. It was almost beyond comprehension. Joy felt the Twizzlers and the soda and the coffee twisting in the pit of her gut as Dr. Carson glanced through the window from the hallway. Noticing the flashing lights, she stepped back into the room, her phone pinned to her ear as she studied the monitors.

"You'll need to mobilize everything you have." Her voice was firm, not betraying the nervous panic bubbling up among the scientists in the room. She waited a moment; then she shook her head, not happy with the response from the other end of the line. "National Guard, Emergency Response . . . the *Pony Express*. We'll meet them down there, but we need all the help we can get."

Dr. Carson ended her call and marched back to the hallway. Joy watched with the rest of the room as she thumbed a quick message into her phone. "That was the vice president," Dr. Carson finally said, the red lights flashing across her face. "She's arranging for a military escort. Wheels up in ten minutes."

Joy did the math in her head.

It was a two-hour flight from Washington, DC, to the Gulf Coast. If Valerie was going to hit—and she was *definitely* going to hit—that would give them eight hours before she made landfall. When it came to BDDs, eight hours was practically a lifetime. If Valerie didn't pick up speed over the Gulf of Mexico, they'd have enough time to coordinate last-minute evacuations with local officials and to help advise as more accurate readings came in.

To make sure as many people lived through Valerie as possible.

"You heard the lady," Joy said, surveying the room.

They were a miserable bunch, red-eyed and runny-nosed. If they had any other job, they'd be home in bed. But they were the NCRC, and boots on the ground was part of the job. Swallowing her nausea, Joy crumpled her empty coffee cup into a ball and tossed it into the trash. A green army helicopter was already making its descent into the adjoining parking lot. In five minutes, they'd all be expected to be onboard and en route to Joint Base Andrews, where an air force pilot was waiting to transport them to a naval air station just outside of New Orleans, Louisiana.

They'd have two hours in the air to catch up on sleep. After that, they had work to do.

NEW ORLEANS

JUNE 11—9:15 A.M.

Emily shaded her eyes as she stepped beneath the trees.

At some point during her long walk from the grocery store, the clouds had cleared, blown by the approaching storm. In their place: the blank canvas of an endless sky, crisp and crystalline blue. Emily shivered as the leaves rustled overhead, wishing she'd thought to bring a hoodie. But there was no planning for this kind of weather. Even in the shadows, the light was strange—overcast and bright at the same time.

Unsure of itself.

Sensing that he was close to his watery home, the turtle shifted in Emily's backpack, slowly rearing onto his hind legs. Stretching toward the parted zipper with his wrinkled neck. *"Shhh,"* Emily whispered, rolling her shoulders so he tumbled back to the bottom of her bag. Apart from a young man playing with his daughter on the swings, the playground was empty. Emily watched them from a distance, frowning as the little girl screeched and kicked her chubby legs toward the sun while the man scrolled through his phone with his free hand.

There was something . . . *off* about the rhythmic squeaking of the rusted swing.

The way it echoed through the oaks gave Emily goose bumps.

She listened for one minute, and then another, until she was finally distracted by a maintenance truck trundling around the bend in the track. She hopped onto the wide stone lip of a nearby fountain for a better look. There wasn't much to see. The driver's sunburnt arm dangled from his open window, his fingers drumming on the weathered door. Unlike most days, there were no cyclists or joggers circling the track, so his foot was on the gas when he veered off the road and onto the grass. A cloud of dust trailed behind him as he disappeared onto the rolling turf of the golf course.

As if on cue, a flock of grackles exploded from the upper branches of a nearby tree, black shadows darting in formation against the cloudless sky. It was only after they shimmered and faded into the distance that Emily realized what was wrong. It wasn't that there were so few people in the park. That was weird, especially on a Sunday morning, but even more unsettling was that there were no squirrels wrestling in the canopy overhead. No sparrows hopping in the grass; no ducklings nipping at her ankles, begging for bread. The grackles were the first birds she'd seen all morning, and they were flying away as fast as they could.

Tiptoeing around the fountain, Emily peered into the whispering leaves above her head for signs of life—but there were only branches, waving in the wind. She wondered if her goose was gone too. If he could manage to fly with his injured wing or if he was stuck in the park with no place to go.

Like Emily.

The girl on the swing started crying.

Emily didn't blame her.

As the wind picked up, blowing swirls of fine pollen across the tall grass, Emily wiped her nose and sniffled at the horizon. Beyond the tree line and the streetcar tracks and the cathedral spires, the perfect blue sky had started to curdle. Emily felt the change more than saw it. From where she was standing, Hurricane Valerie was just a smudge of gray working its way across the Gulf of Mexico—barely visible to the naked eye, even if you knew what to look for.

Emily rubbed the goose bumps from her arms.

She *didn't* know what to look for.

It was obvious that the city was in for more than just a little rain, like her mother absentmindedly predicted— like she *hoped,* despite all signs to the contrary. But Emily was used to summer thunderstorms. If she hadn't been kicked out of her own room, she would have looked forward to the sound of raindrops running down her windows while she read, safe and dry on her cluttered bed. And if she had known just how hard the rain was going to fall, Emily would have sprinted home and dragged her mom and brother down the stairs, into their waiting car.

Germs or no germs.

They'd be halfway to higher ground by now.

Instead, Emily jumped from the lip of the fountain, landing noisily in its basin. The fountain was dry, shut off in anticipation of the coming storm, and she kicked her way through a thick layer of green pennies and shiny dimes as she waited for a sneeze that never came. *Wishing coins.* She thought about picking through them for quarters, but it felt like bad luck to take wishes from the fountain. It wasn't so long ago that Emily had thrown penny after penny into the dark green water herself, praying for a miracle.

And she'd gotten one, more or less.

Elliot was going to be okay.

Emily just hoped that *she* was going to be okay, too.

The giant wind chimes hummed ominously in the distance as the father—sensing rain—carried his daughter to their car. She screeched and squealed, fat tears rolling down her cheeks, and Emily sighed, remembering her mother's book. It was bad enough that she had left it in the park overnight, but if it turned into a pulpy mess, too, that would be just her luck. The strawberry milk and cherry pie settled uncertainly in Emily's stomach as she climbed out of the fountain.

It wasn't hard to retrace her steps.

She knew exactly where she'd hidden from the boys with the cigarettes.

When she closed her eyes, she could almost perfectly picture the cluster of clovers she'd sat in. The grass blurred underfoot as she jogged toward the empty track and then crossed it, her untied laces trailing behind her. It felt good to run, and as she neared the water, her heart lightened. *Everything's going to be okay,* she thought, feeling suddenly like her old self. She didn't know why or how, but she trusted the feeling: *everything's going to be okay.* When Emily reached the clovers, though—the same flowering clovers she could picture so perfectly— her book was nowhere to be found.

Instead, she was greeted by her old friend: the Canada goose.

He untucked his beak from his chest and blinked at Emily as she wrinkled her nose.

"Hi," she said, kneeling to look him in the eye. The two of them were alone on the banks of the lagoon, she realized. The rest of the geese had sensed the storm and fled, but Emily's goose, with his twisted wing, had been left to fend for himself.

He ruffled his feathers reproachfully and Emily found herself apologizing.

"I had to leave," she said. "But I can't be with my family now, either."

The goose shifted his weight, ignoring her.

As he settled into the grass, Emily saw something flash beneath his snowy undercarriage. She reached out slowly—*carefully*—and pressed against the goose, pushing him gently from his roost. His feathers were stiff and unyielding—not soft at all, like she'd thought they'd be—and he preened them back into place as he shuffled toward the muddy banks and back, clucking unhappily. Emily laughed out loud when she saw what he'd been sitting on.

It was streaked with mud and rimmed with feathers . . .

But her mother's book was right where Emily had left it.

Her goose had kept it safe for her.

Sort of.

She wiped the cover on her shorts as the first drops of rain began to fall. Shielding her eyes, Emily looked up in time to see a rogue cloud speeding overhead. It wasn't alone. Two or three others joined it—gray smears against the otherwise cloudless sky. Across the lagoon, the tiny island danced in the wind while Emily considered her options.

She couldn't go home, not yet.

Not with her mom so worked up about Elliot.

But she couldn't stay in the park, either. Not if there was going to be a thunderstorm. She sat heavily on the dew-wet grass, sliding her backpack onto her lap as Spanish moss fluttered in the branches. The turtle blinked mournfully when she pulled him out of her bag, replacing him with her goose-warmed copy of *My Side of the Mountain*.

She slipped it into the padded computer pouch, for extra safety.

"*You* can go home if you want to," Emily said, feeling guilty about keeping her turtle from his turtle friends. She was sad that her brother hadn't met him, but considering everything, it was probably for the best. She turned the turtle's shell so he faced the lagoon and watched him take one tentative step toward the water . . . then turn around. He stared at Emily as the goose leaned into her lap and rested his algae-encrusted beak against her dirty knees. But Emily was too distracted to notice. Another cloud was passing overhead and she'd craned her neck skyward to track it. The turtle crawled slowly into her bag as she shielded her eyes from the rain.

Emily smiled and ripped a handful of clovers from the ground.

She tossed them into her backpack, like confetti, then checked her phone as thunder rumbled in the distance. Her battery was down to three percent, but for once in her life, Emily had messages. Two voice mails from her mother and five missed calls. Also from her mother. Emily's finger hovered over the little red notifications, but she didn't want to listen to them. She couldn't make herself, and she didn't have to—she already knew why her mom was freaking out: she'd finally called Katie's parents and found out that Emily wasn't with them.

That Emily wasn't with *anybody.*

She texted Elliot instead of returning the calls.

"Is everything okay at home?" she asked, typing with one thumb as she chewed the nail of the other. Her phone started ringing almost as soon as she sent the message.

It was her brother.

"Hey," he said, sounding breathless and rushed. "Where are you?"

Emily shrugged, ignoring the question.

"Is Mom still crying or is she angry now?"

"She's not happy, but, Em—"

"Tell her not to worry about me," Emily said.

She pet the goose's head as it nuzzled against her shorts.

"I'm in the park with some new friends and we're having fun, okay?"

"Wait," Elliot interrupted. "Emily, this is important."

They both stopped talking long enough for Emily to hear her mom arguing with someone over the television in the background. She couldn't tell who she was shouting at—if it was her dad or her aunt or some other poor soul on the other end of the line. And she couldn't tell what they'd done to upset her. But Emily was sure of one thing: for the first time that day, she was glad she wasn't home to witness it.

"You have to come back," Elliot said. "You have to—"

Emily waited for him to finish, but her phone had died.

"She doesn't want me back," Emily said, staring at her own bedraggled face in the mirrored black screen. "Not really." A raindrop splattered on her reflection and she was tempted to cry, but she took a deep breath instead. The trees grew thickly on the tiny island—so thickly she thought she might wait out the rain beneath them.

At least for a little while.

She didn't have anywhere else to go . . . and she had no idea what was coming.

But Emily knew that it wouldn't hurt to have her mom worry about *her* for a change, so she took off her shoes and stood up straight, slinging her backpack over her shoulder as she strode toward the rippling banks of the lagoon. The water was warm on her bare feet, but she trembled as she sank into the silt—the thick mud filling the gaps between her toes. Elsewhere in the city, families loaded their minivans and businesses nailed sheets of plywood across their storefronts, readying for what the local newscasters were expecting to be the biggest hurricane to hit the Gulf Coast in at last a century.

It was so big, they weren't even calling it a hurricane anymore.

They were calling it Megastorm Valerie.

FIVE HUNDRED FEET ABOVE SAN JUAN, PUERTO RICO

"This is as close as we can get without landing!" the helicopter pilot yelled.

His hair whipped in the cross-breeze as he twisted to face the cabin, but nobody looked up. They were too busy staring out the open doors, transfixed by the wreckage below. The pilot shook his head, then turned back to the cockpit. Warning lights flashed orange and yellow across the dashboard and the needle on the altimeter seemed to be stuck at zero. . . .

But they were still airborne.

The pilot tapped the glass gauge of the altimeter with a gloved knuckle.

When the needle refused to budge, he cursed beneath his breath.

It was the pressure systems throwing everything off—he knew that, but there was no avoiding it. Even though conditions inside the eye of the storm were crisp and clear, he was flying blind, and there was no way he'd be able to punch the helicopter through Megastorm Valerie. The bowl of the storm had only grown more defined since they'd taken off, and even if he could somehow weave his way through the updrafts without crashing, the wind shear alone would rip them apart. The pilot craned his neck, scanning the horizon for an exit that didn't exist. The sloped walls stretched into the upper atmosphere, thinning but never quite disappearing.

Unbreachable.

He'd have to tie down back at the base and evacuate with the rest of them.

If they still had time to evacuate.

The pilot watched the cameraman strain against his webbed shoulder straps in the rearview mirror. He was hanging halfway out of the helicopter, his video camera wedged into the crook of his shoulder as he filmed the ragged coast. The pilot shook his head, then cranked the volume on his monitors. "You want me to try to put us down or what?" he asked, his amplified voice crackling loudly in their headsets. "We have ten, maybe fifteen minutes before drop-dead go time."

The cameraman shook his head, his camera still trained on the ground below. His eyes were watering from the wind as he squinted through the viewfinder into the waves, his vision blurred. From so high up, La Perla was just a grid of rooftops. Islands in a gently frothing sea. It looked kind of pretty. Like Venice, the cameraman thought. But without the gondolas.

Up close, it would be another story. . . .

A story they wouldn't be able to tell.

Not yet, anyway.

The helicopter weighed at least five thousand pounds, not counting cargo, and there was no telling what kind of structural damage the houses below had already sustained. To the pilot, they might look like a hundred little landing pads spread out beneath them, but the cameraman had seen enough disaster areas to know that any one of them could crumble under their combined weight.

The cameraman wasn't willing to take that chance.

Every heli and medevac in a hundred-mile radius was already working overtime—and even with an entire fleet running twenty-four hours a day, the first responders wouldn't be able to save everyone in Valerie's path. The numbers just didn't add up, and the last thing the cameraman wanted was to become another person who needed to be saved.

His job was to report the news—not become it.

Besides, he didn't have time to get into any trouble.

The network had arranged for their crew to catch a ride to the mainland with a military transport plane. It was already gassed up and waiting for them at the army garrison at Fort Buchanan, just inland of Old San Juan. The plan was to stay just inches ahead of the whipping, southern tail of the storm. In five hours, they'd be waiting on the banks of the Mississippi River—cameras at the ready. When Valerie came raging through the Gulf of Mexico, tearing her way through the cypress swamps, they'd be there to meet her.

That was the *network's* plan, anyway.

The cameraman's plan was to do everything the executives wanted *and* to stay alive while he was doing it.

He kept his eyes peeled for the white van.

He wasn't stupid.

He knew the boy had taken it, and he had known where the boy was headed, too. Even if the cameraman's phone hadn't been synched with the van's GPS, he had a feeling he'd find the boy in La Perla. He just didn't know *where* in La Perla. The cameraman clenched his teeth as he leaned a little farther over the waves. Tiny whitecaps crested over the upturned belly of a rusted yellow truck.

The cameraman didn't like to admit it to himself, but there was a good chance the white van had met a similar fate.

If that was the case, he hoped the boy wasn't with it.

The rest of the crew shifted in their seats as turbulence shook the helicopter. They listed left and then right before the pilot was able to pull them back into an unsteady hover. Whatever happened, they couldn't stay much longer—the cameraman knew that. He told himself that the boy would be fine if they weren't able to find him. That the boy was resourceful.

He'd driven away with their van, after all.

He'd slipped right past them, beneath their noses.

But he was running out of places to run. The San Juan Pilastro had taken on at least three feet of water since the flooding started. The cameraman had seen a school of grunts and snappers swimming through the lobby with his own eyes, right before they'd packed up their gear and headed out.

And La Perla . . .

Looking down into what was left of the neighborhood, he found it hard to imagine that more was on the way—but the second half of Valerie was expected to be three times more powerful than the first. The NCRC had sent so many alerts about the growing storm that he'd had to turn off his phone to save the battery. And still, with all that warning—with the mandatory evacuations and the National Guard—the boy from the Pilastro was stranded somewhere below them, trapped between the waves.

The cameraman couldn't help but think that he was partly to blame.

If he hadn't brushed him off . . .

If he had just taken a minute to talk with him, the boy might have stayed at the resort and evacuated with the rest of the staff.

But he hadn't, so the cameraman had to at least *try* to find him.

He wouldn't be able to live with himself if he didn't.

To buy some time, he told the rest of the crew that he wanted some extra footage anyway. That they could make a story out of it when they found the boy. "A human-interest segment," he'd explained. "The boy who danced for the cameras, to break up the gloom."

The reporter hadn't been convinced, but the reporter wasn't with them.

He was already on the plane, typing his own name into the browser on his phone. They were the only crew in Puerto Rico when the storm hit, and his broadcasts had been syndicated internationally. His face had been flashed across all the major channels, and he was anxious to know if he was famous yet. The reporter was disappointed to see that nobody was talking about him specifically, but he still had half a hurricane to go. And that wasn't counting the aftermath: the trash-strewn beaches, the crying children.

The reporter took a long tug from a silver flask and smiled as he settled into his seat.

He was going to be on every television set in the world before this was over.

Meanwhile, the cameraman raised a walkie-talkie to his lips, hoping the boy had been smart enough to pull its mate from the van's dashboard.

That he hadn't been swept off the low cliff into the sea.

"Breaker one-nine!" the cameraman shouted into the receiver. "Do you copy?"

While he waited for the boy to answer, he scanned the wall of clouds surrounding the island. Surrounding *him*. It was like nothing he'd ever seen before. They were thick, and moving so quickly they seemed to be writhing. Lightning flashed from deep within the storm—bolt after crackling bolt. From a distance, they looked like fireflies wrapped beneath a suffocating gauze. He stared at the flashing lights, transfixed—tapping his foot on the helicopter's grated floor.

A nervous tic.

A metal floor.

As he stared into the walls of the storm, it occurred to him that the entire helicopter was metal: a tiny lightning rod, bobbing uncertainly in the wind.

Tempting fate.

The cameraman shivered.

No matter what happened, they couldn't spend all day waiting for the boy. Their evacuation window was shrinking—and if they weren't on the tarmac and ready to go in thirty minutes, the plane's pilot wouldn't think twice about leaving without them. Thunder cracked from within the clouds and the air shimmered with anticipation as it unrolled across the sky, booming so loudly the cameraman's shoulder shook.

He steadied the camera, ignoring the sideways glances of the crew while the helicopter pilot struggled with the steering yoke, correcting for a rising crosswind. They didn't want to stay in the air any longer than they had to. Not with the reporter already on the plane and the megastorm tightening its grip on the island.

"C'mon, kid!" the cameraman shouted into the walkie-talkie. "It's now or never!"

—

Five hundred feet below the wind-wracked helicopter, Alejo sat slumped over the kitchen table in Padrino

Nando's apartment. He was the last remaining person in La Perla. He knew that for a fact, without question, because he'd spent the last hour checking the streets to make sure. The streets he could get to, anyway. His clothes were drenched from the flooding, and his shoes dripped rainwater onto the linoleum floor.

Alejo cradled his head in his hands, trying to ignore the moaning wind.

There was a pressure building behind his eyes, and he wanted to cry. But there was no time for crying. He had to think. To figure out what he should do next. He needed to fly away, like Padrino Nando had told him to do in his note—but the van was gone. *Everyone* was gone. And San Juan was an island, after all—wherever he ran, the ocean would be waiting for him.

But he couldn't stay in the apartment; that much was clear.

If he stayed, it would be the last thing he did.

Alejo rolled his thumbs over his closed eyes, pressing down until he saw stars. It seemed impossible that everything had been normal just yesterday—and now, with the wind howling and the walkie-talkie buzzing against the hardwood floor, he could barely hear his own thoughts.

"*Vamos*, Alejo," he whispered, squeezing his eyes shut. "*Think.*"

The walkie-talkie had slipped behind the futon in the

night, jammed between the frame and the mattress. With his entire world falling apart around him, he'd forgotten that he'd taken it in the first place. It wasn't until a break in the wind that Alejo even heard the tiny voice calling to him. He jerked his head toward the living room, goose bumps running up his arms and down his back.

"Pick up, kid," the voice said. "You gotta pick up."

Alejo unclenched his fists.

A way out.

"*¡Aló!*" he yelled, the kitchen chair clattering to the tiles as he scrambled after the sound. Rushing to answer, he pulled the futon mattress to the floor and reached between the slats for the crackling walkie-talkie. It was only when he was cradling it in his trembling hands that he remembered the van. It was gone now, and they'd want to know what happened to it. His face blanched, the static popping as he considered his options.

It didn't take long. . . .

He didn't have any.

"Last chance," the cameraman yelled.

"Someone took your van," he finally said. "They needed it to get out of here."

"The van's not important, kid. We've gotta get you out of there, okay? Tell me, where are you, exactly?"

Alejo rattled off Padrino Nando's address, but it didn't mean much anymore: there weren't really streets now—

not in La Perla. Just broken sidewalks and salt water lapping against the seaweed-strewn stairs.

"Look for the yellow house," he said. "By the yellow truck."

The rhythmic chopping of the helicopter's rotors filled the empty living room as the cameraman activated their channel again. He shouted above the noise, but all Alejo could hear was the chopping of the blades.

He clutched the walkie-talkie to his chest as he walked to the front door.

The sound was coming from outside as well.

It was overhead.

MEGASTORM VALERIE

The little petrel flew for nine hours straight before he stopped to rest.

It wasn't so bad in the eye of the storm, and he'd stayed aloft as long as he could, floating on updrafts and waiting for the clouds to dissipate. But even floating took effort, and his muscles were burning with fatigue by the time he settled down on a massive swell, as far away as he could get from the nearest whitecaps. He was hungry, but the water was too rough to fish, so he sat very still on the surface of the wave, tucking his black legs into the warmth of his body.

Away from currents ripping underfoot.

It felt good to rest.

To close his eyes and block out the wind.

The petrel dipped his beak beneath the dark waves and drank, filling his belly with seawater. He didn't know how lucky he was to be able to drink, at the very least. The other birds who were trapped in Valerie's eye— yellow and red songbirds less accustomed to the open waters—could only survive on fresh water and would have died if they'd done the same.

Some had.

But the petrel just floated on its wave.

A gentle rain began to fall, running down his oily feathers, but the petrel was so exhausted that he barely noticed. The ocean was cold. It reminded him of Antarctica and the rest of his flock. He could almost see them, spinning and diving over the glacial plains. Squawking at the scientist who spoke to him so soothingly. He had no way of knowing that nearly five thousand miles away, the sample she took sat in an industrial freezer in the basement of the ecology building at Københavns Universitet—the University of Copenhagen. The number on the sample corresponded to the number stamped onto the aluminum band wrapped around his webbed foot. He wasn't yet old enough to mate, so if he sank beneath the waves, that would be all that was left of him.

A vial of blood in a basement far from home.

It was only when the rain began to fall harder,

pummeling his head and wings, that the petrel opened his eyes again. Through the rain, he could see the sun shining down into the eye of the hurricane. But he'd waited too long, and he was no longer in the calm blue eye. The swell he'd settled on was fast-moving, and it started to crest as it propelled him deeper into the thick, ragged bands of Valerie's spiral. Visibility was low in the spiral, but the petrel could see that the waves only got rougher beyond the gray haze. He had no choice but to fly. It was either that or be sucked into the surf, battered beneath the watery tonnage of an angry sea.

His stiff feathers ruffled in the wind as he launched himself into the storm. He wasn't strong enough to fly back into the eye, through the megastorm's wall, so he leaned into the spiral instead, letting the updrafts blow him skyward. The updrafts were strong—so strong that he tumbled through the currents, more tossed than flying. For a terrifying moment, before he was able to right himself in the upper reaches of the atmosphere, it seemed as if he might be thrown back down into the waves.

Whether through luck or divine providence, the tiny petrel was spared.

He stretched his wings wide and ignored the pain.

Closing his eyes, he tried to picture the way the sun dazzled in the snow.

He would make it back someday, if the storm would

let him. He was sure of it. He would find his flock and he would nest on the same rocky islet off the frigid shores where he was hatched. But for now, the wind would take the petrel where it wanted. Lightning struck somewhere beneath him, its flashing light swallowed by the darkness of the storm and the roiling sea.

The little petrel paid it no attention.

The air was thin so high up, and the petrel slipped in and out of consciousness as he drifted with the storm.

NEW ORLEANS

JUNE 11—9:30 A.M.

Elliot ran his fingers across his stomach as he listened to his mother argue with Aunt Lillian. The stitches would disappear on their own, dissolving into the scarred and puckered line across his abdomen, the cancer gone. He'd wanted to keep what they'd taken out of him as a souvenir for his bookshelf, in a jar between his Wonder Woman and his Wolverine—but he hadn't been awake to ask the doctors. In fact, he hardly remembered the surgery. It was the fear leading up to it that stuck with him.

And the exhaustion afterward.

He was still tired two weeks later, even though he slept most days.

The medicine was to blame for that.

It made him feel like he was floating underwater, and he hated it almost as much as he hated being sick. He could barely stay awake past the opening credits of a movie, much less catch up on his weekly comic books. The pills were big and blue and made his mouth dry. So dry it hurt to swallow. Elliot took a sip of the orange juice his mom had brought him just before Aunt Lillian called, and palmed the pills she'd set beside the half-filled glass on his bedside table. Saving them for later, when he might really need them. It wouldn't be the end of the world if he skipped a day, he hoped, swinging his legs to the floor.

Inhaling sharply as his feet hit the carpet.

It was bad enough that he'd wasted his entire summer vacation in bed.

It didn't seem fair to hurt so much on top of that.

But Elliot didn't have a choice.

He had to get out of bed and get dressed, for Emily.

The television in the living room was turned up louder than usual and even then, it didn't drown out the neighbors. Above and below their apartment, Elliot could hear them hammering—boarding their windows shut. Preparing for the coming storm. Some had already left, driving north through a predawn haze, and the rest were doing whatever they could to get out before the roads flooded. Elliot gritted his teeth as he dressed, gingerly pulling on an old pair of basketball shorts and a faded red T-shirt.

Slipping his pain pills into his pocket. The scar on his stomach twinged as he tied his shoes, but it was nothing compared to the worry that had started twisting in the bottom of his gut as soon as his sister hung up on him.

It wasn't just their apartment building. . . .

The entire city was packing up, and Emily was outside—alone in the park.

As far as Elliot could tell, she had no idea what was coming.

If she did, she would've been home by now.

Elliot hadn't eavesdropped very long, but he'd listened long enough to know that Aunt Lillian was stuck in traffic. That she was begging them to evacuate, too—to meet her in Arkansas or South Carolina. Away from the storm. The news was saying they had hours—not days—before it reached land, and as much as his mom hated the idea of dragging Elliot out of his sickroom, she didn't need any more convincing. But it was too late. There was no way she could leave their apartment, much less the city. Not while his dad was driving home from the rig, and definitely not before Emily "got her butt back here."

There was nothing she could do but wait.

"Stop shouting," she said.

She was half shouting herself.

"We have time—we'll be gone before it hits."

Elliot wasn't so sure that was true.

He stood with his ear pressed against his bedroom door, listening to the floorboards squeak as his mother paced. It was taking all her willpower not to jump in their car and circle the block, yelling his sister's name from the driver's-side window. He knew because that was what she had threatened to do in the voice mails she'd left Emily before Aunt Lillian called. Elliot sighed. He was glad his mom had decided to hold down the fort instead—to stay put, like they taught in wilderness training. She wouldn't be able to find his sister, anyway. She didn't know where to look, and besides . . .

Somebody had to be home in case Emily came back.

Finally, the bathroom door creaked shut.

His mother was still arguing with Aunt Lillian as she turned on the sink.

"Listen, we'll be there when we can," she said, splashing her face—her exasperation muffled by the running water. "That's just the way it has to be right now." Elliot wasn't so sure about that either, but it was up to him to prove her wrong. His heart raced as he tiptoed past the bathroom, easing his bedroom door shut behind him. Seizing the moment while his mother reached for a hand towel. As he snuck through the living room and out of their apartment—alone, for the first time in months—he almost felt like his old self again.

Almost.

He wasn't jumping down the stairs three at a time—he had to hold on to the banister—but it felt good to be out of his bed and in the world. Elliot smiled as he stepped onto the sidewalk. There weren't many people on the street, but the people he did see were busy. Trucks trundled up the avenue, their reinforced beds weighed down by sheets of plywood. A baby cried in her car seat while her mother loaded their station wagon with plastic jugs of water. A helicopter flew low overhead, its tail emblazoned with the logo from a local news channel.

It wasn't until Elliot had walked a few blocks that he noticed how strangely quiet the city was, despite all the activity. The trolleys weren't running, and he only counted three cars on the road. One was the parked station wagon, the other two were police cruisers. Otherwise, there were no idling engines, no laughter from people waiting for the bus. The air was so still that he could hear the gibbons in the zoo whooping and howling from four blocks away. Their calls echoed through the empty streets as Elliot walked, and he wondered if they were going to be evacuated, too, or if the zoo was just going to leave them there, trapped in their cages.

The old Elliot would have wanted to break them out. To save them, too.

The new Elliot wiped the sweat from his forehead with the back of his arm. He was starting to feel a little queasy, and fresh guilt mixed with the worry in the pit of his stomach. After everything she'd been through, scaring his mom was the last thing he wanted to do. Elliot stopped walking and looked homeward. He wasn't so far away—he could be back in his bedroom in fifteen minutes.

In the distance, the gibbons whooped.

"Come on," Elliot muttered, dialing his sister one last time as he walked beneath the whispering trees. It rang once, then went straight to voice mail. "Hi," Emily said, but it was just a recording. "I don't really listen to these, so just text me, okay?" Elliot frowned as a police cruiser sped past him, flashing red and blue. Another cruiser followed it, joined by a fire engine with its siren blaring. Elliot watched them race down the avenue, barely slowing as they pulled onto the grass of Audubon Park.

He craned his neck to see where they were heading, then flinched as he felt his stitches pull—pinching at the soft skin above his waist. Elliot gripped his side, squeezing his scar so tightly his knuckles whitened, then sat heavily on the sidewalk. The concrete was hot on his bare legs, and his stomach hurt so badly—and so *suddenly*—that all he could do was spit, breathing heavily through his teeth as the pain subsided. He took one deep breath and then another, exhaling as a trio of ants converged on the wet spot at his feet.

"You're all right," he told himself. *"You're going to be all right."*

But there was something about the strange green and yellow cast of the sky that made Elliot feel unsure of himself. Despite the heat, the sun had disappeared behind a wall of gray clouds—and the emergency sirens had quieted, replaced with mournful gibbons. The quiet was unnerving, especially since red and blue lights still flashed from deep within the park. Overhead, the canopy rustled in the rising wind. The trees had lived through more storms than anyone. They were ancient, and their twisted branches arched over the avenue like the ceiling of a cathedral.

"Please let her be okay," Elliot whispered, staring up into the leaves.

He fingered the pills in his pocket, but he couldn't afford to be foggy.

Not now.

"Let me be okay, too," he said, gripping his stomach as he walked toward the flashing lights.

PART THREE

FLYING

You meet the blast, and your little wings bear
you up against it. . . .

—JOHN JAMES AUDUBON, *BIRDS OF AMERICA*,
VOLUME VII, "WILSON'S PETREL"

FORTY FEET ABOVE SAN JUAN, PUERTO RICO

JUNE 11—9:45 A.M.

"Ten feet starboard," the cameraman yelled, loud enough for the pilot to hear him over the chopping blades. "Now five!" It was hard to see the boy through the shaking viewfinder—but he was there, standing on the sinking front porch of the yellow house, squinting up into the rain. The cameraman waved with his free hand as the crew fed a thick nylon rope through the open doors of the helicopter.

It was all they had.

There was no white stretcher strapped to the back wall of the cabin. No climbing net stowed beneath the grated floor. Just a coil of workaday black rope, heavy enough not to whip in average winds.

As far as rescues went, it was far from perfect.

They'd circled La Perla twice looking for a safe place to land, but it was too risky, even with the helicopter's small footprint. They'd even tried farther inland, buzzing low over Old San Juan—inspecting the coast, from the rocky outcropping of the Castillo San Cristóbal to the rolling fields of Punta del Morro. But the damage was widespread on either side of the wall, and there was no telling how many felled power lines were hidden beneath the flooding. Between the wreckage and the mudslides and the rising surf, the cameraman didn't want to risk a landing.

Not with Megastorm Valerie breathing down their necks.

—

Alejo shielded his eyes as he watched the heavy black rope wriggling like a worm from the belly of the helicopter. It was so far up that he couldn't see any faces—just silhouettes: arms feeding the rope into the empty air, dangling it from the open door. His heart was racing, but he wasn't scared to hang on to the loop they'd knotted into the bottom of the rope. To swing out over the cresting waves. He just wished Padrino Nando could see him. . . .

That he could know that Alejo was taking his advice after all.

That he was flying away.

Away from the house he loved and away from his *padrino*—who would be worried sick, Alejo realized, when he came back to look for him. While the helicopter adjusted, hovering ten feet to the right and then forward—positioning itself as close to Alejo as possible— he sprinted back inside, jumping over a capsized chair on his way to the cupboard. Nando had a chipped coffee mug full of pens that he kept there, next to his stationery. Alejo uncapped one, conscious of the walkie-talkie buzzing on the table beside him. He didn't have much time, so he grabbed the first thing that came to hand: a birthday card, one of many his *padrino* had been saving and would likely never send.

"I can't see you," the cameraman shouted. "Where'd you go?"

Alejo scrawled a quick note in the card, then slipped it into a sandwich bag, like Nando had done before him. Rushing as fast as he could, Alejo pulled open the junk drawer beside the sink—looking for tape, so his message wouldn't blow away. He pulled so hard the drawer derailed from its tracks, spilling its contents onto the floor. Dead batteries rolled across the tiles and clipped recipes fluttered to his feet.

But there was no tape.

The walkie-talkie continued to buzz as Alejo stared wild-eyed around the kitchen.

He couldn't leave the card on the table, unattached.

"Kid, we don't have time to play games here."

Alejo agreed.

His *padrino*'s weathered knife was heavy in his pocket.

He'd wanted to hold on to it, to keep it safe for Nando—but he flicked it open instead. The blade was short and polished, used mostly to pare oranges. Sweet *chinas,* Padrino Nando's favorite. He turned them slowly in his hands so their thick skin came off in one long piece. Raising the tiny knife aloft, Alejo jammed it through the center of the sandwich bag and into the soft blond wood of the kitchen table. *"Feliz cumpleaños!"* the front of the card read. *Happy birthday.* Beneath the rainbow-colored greeting was a picture of a teddy bear holding a balloon bouquet. The bear looked a little squeamish to Alejo, but he'd been spared.

The Mylar balloons hadn't been so lucky.

Alejo wiggled the weathered handle and smiled.

The knife didn't budge.

"I'm still here," he shouted, gripping the walkie-talkie against his cheek as he ran back outside. The helicopter was hovering directly overhead, so low that it was making its own waves, and the rope danced over the water just a few feet out from Padrino Nando's front porch. All Alejo had to do was grab the rope and he'd be saved, but as soon as he jumped across the threshold, the porch gave way beneath him. The storm clouds blurred into the surf as he fell, his legs throbbing with the hot red insistence of freshly skinned knees.

Blinking back at the doorway, Alejo tried to understand what had thrown him.

But there was nothing to see, just the front door bobbing gently in the waves.

Only, it wasn't Padrino Nando's door that was bobbing.

It was the porch, rolling like a docked raft.

Unmoored by the flooding.

The walkie-talkie slipped into the backwash of the encroaching sea and Alejo's heart sank along with it. His wrist ached sharply beneath his chest. He'd fallen on it wrong, and he was worried that it was broken. That he wouldn't be able to hold on to the rope. But there was no time to second-guess himself. The turbulence from the helicopter's spinning blades was so strong that he stumbled as he climbed to his feet, cradling his wrist against his chest. His scrapes stung in the wind, but Alejo bit the inside of his cheek and pushed on. . . .

Inching toward the water.

"C'mon, kid!"

The cameraman leaned out of the helicopter's open door as he shouted, his voice hoarse in the wind. He was close enough that he didn't need the walkie-talkie, but far enough away that he had to yell for Alejo to hear him over the crashing waves.

"Grab the rope!"

Despite its weight, the rope snaked back and forth in the wash of the helicopter's rotors, five feet from the lip of the porch. Alejo stared at the loop tied into its bottom and at the rising tides beneath it. Since he'd been awake, the waves had worked their way up past the sidewalk and over the rear wheels of Padrino Nando's truck. He watched them break above its rusted tail, pulled by invisible tides and currents, and—taking a deep breath—backed against the door. From the helicopter, it looked like he was giving up, but Alejo was determined to fly.

He just needed a running start.

Balancing on the porch, Alejo cradled his wrist—his legs acclimating to the roll of the sea. *"Vamos, vamos, vamos,"* he told himself, swallowing a growing fear.

"Just . . . *go!*"

Time didn't stop as Alejo ran to the lip of the porch and leapt.

It didn't even slow.

He felt himself grasping for the rope almost as soon as his feet left the porch, but it was smoother than he expected and slick with rain. It slapped against Alejo's cheek as he hugged it to his chest, gripping it as tightly as he could with his good hand. *Clutching it.* The cameraman yelled encouragements as he slipped down to the loop, but they hardly registered. Beneath Alejo's kicking feet, the porch was pulling away from the house—tipping precariously into the crashing waves as the helicopter drifted slowly upward.

The longer he held on, the farther he would fall if he let go.

And with every passing second, he was farther from the sea.

"You can do this," Alejo whispered through gritted teeth, punching his broken wrist through the loop. He pretzeled around the rope as it swayed back and forth across the water—locking himself into place just in time. The rope spun wildly as the crew pulled him skyward, slamming Alejo against the side of Nando's house, then swinging him over the waves in a wide arc. Alejo didn't scream or shut his eyes as he smashed against the gutter of a nearby roof. Instead, he stared up at the helicopter, squinting against the rain.

Trying to make himself as small and light as possible.

The nylon chafed against his wrist, and he could feel it swelling. But he didn't care.

He'd made it.

"We got you, kid," the cameraman shouted.

Lightning flashed over the Atlantic, casting his wolf-ish grin in a sickly green light.

"Hold on!"

The cameraman strained as he pulled him into the open door by his armpits, the nylon rope falling into a limp pile at his boots. As soon as Alejo was safely in the helicopter, the cameraman grasped the back of his head, staring into his eyes. "Are you okay?" he asked, looking for the spark he had seen the night before, when Alejo had given him the pint of melted ice cream. Alejo just blinked, the blood from his skinned knees mixing with the rain running down his legs. He was shaking with shock and adrenaline and holding his arm like a broken wing, crooked delicately across his chest. He needed a hospital, but that would have to wait.

The bowl of the storm was tightening. . . .

The clouds on the horizon growing larger by the minute.

"It's okay," the cameraman said, softening his gruff voice into a comforting growl. "I've got you," he repeated, as much to himself as to the Alejo. "You're safe."

Alejo just nodded, holding his tongue.

He was grateful to have been picked up by the camera crew and was sorry that their van was missing. He wanted to apologize . . . but it was better to say nothing, he thought, than to bring it up and risk upsetting every-one after everything they'd done for him. The helicopter pitched forward as the cameraman guided Alejo to a free seat and buckled him in.

The pilot wasn't taking any chances.

He had already pointed the helicopter toward Fort Buchanan and was flying it as fast as it would go. "No time for a drop-off," he announced, activating the crack-ling intercom. He sounded calm and in charge, but the intercom stayed on as he mumbled encouragements to himself—unaware of his terrified audience.

The cameraman squeezed Alejo's shoulder. "We'll get you back to your family," he said, shouting to be heard over the whining engines. "Later, after the storm."

Alejo nodded and leaned against his straps, strain-ing for a look at La Perla through the open doors, but he couldn't see much. An impenetrable fog crept below them, and he could just barely make out the faded gray line of Calle Norzagaray as they flew inland. Once they were over land again, it started raining—so hard it sounded like the helicopter would be drowned out of the sky.

Alejo clutched his throbbing wrist.

He didn't know where they were going, but they were flying over San Juan and he couldn't even see the island to say goodbye. In the distance, the jagged smudge of a

mountain range poked up above the clouds. The Cordil-
lera Central, where Nando had been evacuated—driven
in a crowded bus by the National Guard to a high school
auditorium in Barranquitas.

He was safe now, Alejo told himself.

For the time being, they both were.

VENICE, LOUISIANA

Silas and the rest of P7 Beta's skeleton crew had landed at the heliport in Venice, Louisiana, in the small hours of the night, officially abandoning their rig to the coming storm. Tacked onto the southernmost tip of the state, Venice was a funny place: a fading freckle above the mouth of the Mississippi River that was, at three in the morning, completely deserted. Silas had been too tired to make the drive home in the dark, so he'd curled up on the front bench of his truck with the windows down, a stone's throw from the river and so close to the Gulf of Mexico that he could almost hear the coast eroding as he tried to drift into sleep.

It hadn't come easily.

Silas had twisted fitfully on his makeshift bed, his knees knocking against the dashboard. It made it hard to relax, knowing that one good wave could wipe him off the map. That if Valerie came in hard, he could be the last person to spend the night in a truck on the side of LA-23, listening to the cattle egrets gossip in the reeds. He'd texted his wife to let her know that he'd be home as soon as he could and stared into the twinkling blackness beyond his bug-flecked windshield, waiting for an answer.

Seven hours later, he woke with a start.

The sun hadn't risen, not properly.

The horizon was just a gray haze, and Silas had no idea how late he'd slept until he answered his ringing phone. "Hey," he said, rubbing the sleep from his eyes as his wife muted the news in their apartment. "How's everyone?"

Silas stretched and stared into the distance as she filled him in. Her sister Lillian was halfway to Arkansas. She was begging them to join her, and everyone in their building had already evacuated. But his daughter, Emily, wasn't answering her phone. *His* daughter—it wasn't like her. Silas frowned as a flock of brown pelicans flew low over the marsh, circling archipelagos of cane and tall grass in search of mullet and minnows.

Breakfast.

"It's a what?" he said, his stomach growling and knotting at the same time.

The last time Silas had checked, Valerie was still a Category 3 hurricane—strong enough to force an evacuation of the rig, but just barely more than a tropical storm. At some point in the night, she'd been upgraded into a full-blown disaster. It was news to him. Silas turned his key in the ignition and pulled his truck onto the highway, its all-terrain tires spitting clamshell gravel in his wake.

"A *megastorm*," he repeated, whistling through his teeth. "Hang tight," he said. "I can be home in an hour."

Silas pressed his steel-toed boot against the gas, then scanned the radio frequencies until he found the emergency alert station. Based on projections from the National Climatic Research Center, FEMA (Federal Emergency Management Agency) had issued a preemptive call for first responders. They needed people with experience in a crisis. People who could be helpful when push came to shove. The address they gave for their pre-storm headquarters made Silas sweat into his collar. Volunteers were being asked to meet in a series of soccer fields in Audubon Park, in the center of the city—so after six days of twelve-hour shifts on the sweltering rig, Silas was headed home . . .

To ground zero.

If the roads stayed clear, he told himself, they could still make it to Arkansas.

He'd just have to gun it.

Silas flipped to a rhythm-and-blues station, the crosswind roaring as he switched into a higher gear. The music didn't match his mood, but he hardly noticed. His daughter was AWOL and every building he passed— every diner and bar and two-bit motel—was boarded up for the storm. *The megastorm.* Silas clenched his teeth, his jaw squaring as the speedometer climbed above seventy miles an hour and then eighty. He was driving too fast for the road, kicking loose rocks up against the undercarriage of his truck.

But Silas didn't have a choice.

His family needed him.

—

Joy practically tumbled out the rear door of the government-issue SUV. She caught herself before she slipped on the grass, her tennis shoes sticking in the mud. The air was so humid her hair frizzed on contact, but she took a deep breath anyway—filling her lungs. The flight from Washington had been awful, and not because of the turbulence.

Bumps she could handle.

It was the coughing that had gotten to her.

Her colleagues—the alpha force of disaster preparedness—had gone through two boxes of tissues and a bag of maximum-strength lozenges on the short drive from the airfield in Venice to the emergency response headquarters in Audubon Park, but it hadn't helped. They were so sick they could barely keep their eyes open. It was more than Joy could say for herself. She was exhausted, too, but with all the sneezing, she hadn't been able to get any sleep on the plane.

And the germs.

She shivered beneath the oaks just thinking about them.

Inside the SUV, Dr. Abigail Carson snored on Rob's shoulder as he drooled against the glass. Joy watched the window fog and smiled. They were out cold, and she wasn't about to wake them. It was going to be a long day, and her job was only going to be easier without the director sniffling down her neck. She closed the car door as gently as she could and tiptoed to the nearest police officer.

"Joy Harrison," Joy whispered, tapping the officer on the shoulder. "NCRC. Who's in charge here?"

NEW ORLEANS

JUNE 11—12:00 P.M.

While the rest of the city evacuated, Emily pulled herself onto the lowest limb of a gnarled oak. From there, it was an easy climb to her new hideaway: a sheltered nest at the heart of the tree, where three thick branches forked and folded in on each other. Emily felt protected in the twist of their ancient arms, shaded by gossamer curtains of Spanish moss. *Completely oblivious.* With her phone's battery dead, she had no way of knowing that the storm had been upgraded. Or that she was sitting in a state of emergency. It was drizzling, but the tree kept her as dry as if she'd been in her own bedroom—and it was so much better than skulking around the streets in the rain, working up the nerve to go back home.

To face her mother.

It was perfect.

So perfect that Emily hadn't wanted to climb down . . . but she'd needed to go to the bathroom for over an hour and she couldn't wait any longer. She scrambled down the trunk, upsetting the goose, who had been napping between the loosely braided roots with his legs tucked beneath his downy chest. He shuffled nervously after Emily as she made her way to a dense cluster of cattails. She could feel him blinking at her as she peered through the reeds.

"Shoot," she whispered, watching the lagoon ripple with raindrops.

The weather was taking a turn for the worse and she'd left her book next to her backpack, propped in a cache of brown leaves and dried acorns twenty feet above the ground. Emily peed as fast as she could, then sprinted back to the tree, where she swung herself up through the branches like one of the gibbons in the zoo.

Racing against the rain.

She needn't have worried.

The storm battered the outer crown of the tree, but the trunk was dry and soft, the layered canopy impervious to the rain. Its leaves whispered all around Emily, shimmering in the wind as she settled back into the curve of the oak and brushed a cluster of pollen from her mom's old book. It had been through a lot since Emily had started reading it, and she wasn't even halfway done. She ran her finger down a dog-eared page, finding where she'd left off and picking up again, but she couldn't focus.

She was too sad and too anxious.

And too angry.

It wasn't right that she had nowhere to go.

That she had to hide in a tree on a swampy little island while rain clouds gathered overhead. The unfairness of it simmered in Emily's veins, the steam rising and crowding her thoughts as she tried to read the same paragraph three times in a row. But the words barely registered, and when she tried to read it through a fourth time, she was distracted by the chimes.

The way they jangled in the rain sounded lonesome.

They reminded her of her mother.

Of everything they'd been through together.

Emily stared up into the leaves, her eyes swimming with swaying patterns of light and dark as she tried to fight back tears. A fat carpenter ant crawled across her arm and a squirrel chittered somewhere below as she matched her breath to the wind: inhaling and exhaling as the trees danced in the rain. Inhaling . . .

And exhaling.

There was a hole in the tree beside Emily's perch—a

hand-sized hollow stuffed with fallen sticks and leaves. She absentmindedly cleared it, tossing the dried foliage out into the rain as she dug. The hole went back a good foot into the trunk, where it expanded into a natural safe—dry and secret. *Protected.* Emily brushed the chamber clean with the palm of her hand, then scanned her tree for other hidden treasures.

For handholds and pathways, for when she brought Elliot.

With his help, she could turn the little island into a full-blown fort, with hammocks and pulleys and everything. Emily wiped the tears from her cheeks and climbed higher into the boughs, taking stock of the twisting angles and wondering if she could branch out into neighboring trees. If there was a way to bridge them. She was vaguely aware of a brewing excitement in Audubon Park as she worked her way through the canopy, but the muffled sirens and distant voices made her feel safe, not scared.

Like she wasn't alone after all.

Beneath her, at the foot of the tree, her goose settled back down between the knotted roots. Emily could just barely see his black tail twitching from her perch. She smiled, then reached into her backpack to pat her turtle's mossy shell. It was impossible to read the expression on his leathery face, but he seemed content to stare at her as she worked. Emily shivered as she pulled herself onto an even higher limb. Not because she was cold, but because she was full and she was dry and she was happy.

If just for a little while . . .

FORTY THOUSAND FEET ABOVE THE NORTH ATLANTIC OCEAN

Alejo sat cradling his arm in the belly of a matte gray C-40 Clipper, a reinforced tank of a plane that was putting as much distance as possible between itself and Megastorm Valerie. The Clipper was a military jet, so there were no frills and no snack carts, but the cameraman had found him a can of soda, anyway—a Diet Coke from the pilot's private stash.

Alejo sipped it slowly as they hurtled over the Atlantic. Making it last.

There was a nervous energy on the plane, an excitement that felt wrong after what had happened to La Perla. Alejo could feel it rippling through the cabin as he sat quietly in his seat, trying to ignore the engine roaring just outside his window. He'd started out leaning against the double-paned glass, transfixed by the curve of the earth receding into the distance, but it was his first time on a plane. For all his talk about flying away, Alejo had drawn the shade halfway through takeoff to help fight his growing nausea.

The painkillers weren't helping.

Back at the base, a medic had given him something for his wrist—along with a splint and an oversized sling. The sling he'd double-knotted around Alejo's shoulder, the pill he'd cut in half . . . but it was still too much. Alejo could feel it turning in his stomach, agitated by the bubbles in his drink. He swallowed a burp as a man in a pressed blue uniform hustled toward the cockpit behind a woman in fatigues: the soldier who had helped him onto the plane when he'd almost fainted on the tarmac, waiting to board.

He'd needed to sit.

To lie down on the polished concrete.

But he'd leaned heavily onto the soldier's arm instead. She'd asked about his parents, and Alejo had tried to answer—to explain about Padrino Nando and his mother in the States—but his mouth felt like it was full of cotton.

"What's that, sweetie?" the soldier had said, not unkindly, but she'd been distracted.

Everyone had been doing their job—shouting into phones and walkie-talkies.

Rushing to beat the storm.

A little boy on the airstrip was the least of their priorities.

As she led him up the stairs and to his seat, Alejo had wanted to ask if she knew where the evacuees had been taken and when they'd be back in La Perla. But by the time he got the words out, she was already gone. It was like he was invisible. Nobody on the plane seemed to notice him, and nobody thought to tell him where they were going. They were all too busy. The cameraman and his crew had rushed into the hangar and onto the tarmac, and—except for the soda—he'd been swept up and forgotten in their wake.

It wasn't that they meant to ignore him, Alejo knew that.

They just needed to be airborne before the megastorm hit.

"We'll figure everything out later," the cameraman had said.

But Alejo didn't want to wait for later, so he kept his ears pricked as they flew, listening for clues and swallowing the bile creeping up the back of his throat. The plane was on its way to New Orleans, a city at the very bottom of the United States. That was where everyone thought Valerie was going to make landfall, and they were expecting her to be big.

Bigger than she had been in San Juan.

That was why the news crew was on board.

The rest of the passengers were officers and military personnel. Alejo could tell from their uniforms and from their way of talking—clipped and official and heavy on the acronyms, like they were speaking in code. He didn't know exactly *why* the army was rushing into the storm, as if it were something they could fight. . . .

But they seemed confident, like they knew what they were doing.

Alejo wished he could feel the same way as he watched the man three seats in front of him lean into the aisle, joking with a passing officer. He couldn't hear what the man said, but he would recognize the reporter anywhere. Alejo stared at the back of his ear, wondering if he knew what exactly they were flying into—and if they were going to make it out okay. The reporter just scrolled through his phone, taking an occasional sip from a silver flask, until he finally felt Alejo's eyes boring into his over-gelled hair.

He turned around, scowling, and Alejo hugged himself with his good arm.

It was cold on the plane, and the ice-cold soda made it even colder.

HIGHWAY 23

Torrential rain pounded against the windshield, so hard that Silas couldn't see the road. He swerved to avoid the median, gripping the steering wheel with whitening knuckles as he spat. Cursing at his own bad luck. The skies had been clear when he'd pulled onto the highway and he'd been breaking the speed limit for thirty minutes straight, but it didn't matter. Valerie was catching up to him. With no trees or traffic blocking its way, the storm whipped off the bayou and buffeted his truck until the steering wheel jerked in his hands—shying away from the wind, like a frightened rabbit.

Silas would have pulled over and parked right then if he'd had a choice.

If it had been a normal summer squall instead of a megastorm...

He leaned forward to adjust his windshield wipers instead, but there was no higher setting. They were already working at top speed and struggling to keep up. Silas ran his fingers through his thinning brown hair and sighed. It was impossible to see the bay through the rain, and yet—even with the windows shut and the air conditioner on full blast—the sound of the waves crashing against weathered piers filled his truck. As long as he stayed his course, he knew he could outrun the storm, but it was hard not to second-guess himself when there weren't any other cars on the road.

At least, none that he could see.

Silas frowned.

His eyes were strained and he could've used a strong cup of coffee, but there was no telling when that would happen. There was no telling anything. If he could have just called his wife again, he would have felt better, but his phone was propped in a cup holder—fully charged and as useless as the wipers. He'd lost reception as soon as the rain picked up, and visibility was so low that the occasional flash of reflective yellow paint in his headlights was the only thing guiding him. That and the rhythmic thump his tires made as they ran over thick seams of tar in the asphalt.

Ba-dum, ba-dum, ba-dum, Silas thought. *Like the Jaws music.*

Silas turned the radio on and flipped through the channels, searching for a trace of news in the static. Searching for *anything.* None of the FM stations came through, so he switched to AM with his eyes still on the road, trained for flashes of yellow in the gray. Except for two signals—a bluegrass station and a call-in show—it was all white noise. Silas stopped on the call-in show, hoping for a break in programming or an emergency alert. The show was pretaped, but he kept the radio on anyway, turning up the volume as he peered into the rain. Out of the corner of his eye, through the relentless blur of the storm, he spotted something in his rearview mirror.

Something that made his heart stop.

Silas took a deep breath and fumbled with his phone.

He knew he didn't have any bars, but he kept trying regardless.

"Come *on,*" he said, staring into the massive cloud-banks building over the bayou behind him. It was a wall of gray, like static on the radio, and he didn't want to be anywhere near it when it touched down on the coast. If he had been able to get through to his wife, he would have told her to run—to take Elliot and find Emily and drive as fast as she could. To meet Aunt Lillian in Arkansas and to do it quick. But his phone didn't work, not anymore—not when he needed it. Silas tossed it onto the passenger seat as he stomped on the gas, his tires spitting mud back into the approaching storm as the speedometer jumped from eighty to a hundred miles per hour.

NEW ORLEANS

JUNE II—I:00 P.M.

Taking advantage of a break in the rain, Elliot stepped out from beneath the trees and circled the field of low-slung tents that had been pitched over the course of the morning. He tried to look confident, like he had a reason for being there, but it wasn't easy. Almost everyone else was wearing a uniform, and he was the only kid in sight. Elliot had never seen anything like it. Between the flashing lights and the emergency workers shouting to be heard over rumbling generators, the park was like a movie set.

Except here, the danger was real.

Megastorm Valerie was headed straight for them.

And Emily was nowhere to be found.

Elliot threaded his way between two fire engines, keeping to the shadows as he peeked beneath them—looking for his sister. She'd said she was playing with friends in the park, so he knew she was *somewhere*. He just didn't know where, exactly, and the path around Audubon Park was almost two miles long. Long enough that Elliot was sweating from his search efforts, his stitches straining beneath his shirt.

"Governor's on the line, Joy," someone shouted.

"Do we have a situation report?"

Elliot flattened against one of the trucks, hiding in plain sight as a young woman in a wrinkled blazer and dirty white Converse hustled past him. Luckily for Elliot, she was too busy tapping on her phone to see his skinny arms splayed awkwardly across the bright red metal. Exhaling, he watched her disappear beneath the flaps of a nearby tent, his hand hovering protectively over his side. The last thing he needed was to be caught sneaking around the encampment. . . .

For one of the lingering uniforms to escort him home, to safety.

Emily would have felt the same way.

Wherever she was, she would have hidden as soon as the tents went up.

Elliot was sure of it. That's why he had kept his distance from the makeshift base all morning. While police cars crisscrossed the bustling fields, he'd crept around the less trafficked fringes of the park, stealthily checking all their usual hangouts: the playgrounds and the fence by the zoo. The dusty embankments beneath the mildewed stone bridges. He'd even looped around the lagoon twice, scanning the reeds that lined its muddy shores.

Fighting a rising panic.

He'd been trudging through the rain and mud all morning and except for a handful of turtles and one lonely goose, Elliot hadn't seen any signs of life. The goose had honked at him from across the water, and—feeling suddenly light-headed—Elliot had taken a deep breath, and then another, as giant wind chimes danced in the twisted branches above his head. It was only after his heart stopped pounding in his ears that he'd thought to check his messages from the previous night.

To look for clues in the blurry pictures Emily had sent him.

The mossy turtle on her floor, gnawing on a tangled cord.

A series of tilted selfies, each one blurrier than the last.

Elliot had pinched the screen above Emily's shoulders, zooming in on fuzzy leaves. Straining to see some landmark in the selfies that would help him find his little sister. To find *something* he might recognize in the pixels behind her messy hair. A statue in the distance; a tree that looked familiar somehow. But his fingers—slick with sweat—smudged the screen, and the photos were out of focus to begin with. Emily could have taken them anywhere, and Elliot had looked everywhere he could think of . . .

Everywhere except the one place he'd been so careful to avoid.

—

The wind picked up as Elliot leaned against the fire engine, whipping gusts of rain and pollen through the narrow corridor. Elliot sneezed, doubling over from the effort, then sneezed again—so hard it was like a punch to the gut. He wiped a tendril of spittle from his chin, his hand trembling with shock, then counted to ten and waited for the pain to subside. He reached eleven and then twenty, but Elliot could still feel his stitches pulling on his waist.

Pinching.

Like a scalpel, he thought, blanching as he slid to the ground.

Elliot closed his eyes and concentrated on his breathing.

"You're okay," he whispered, clutching his side—afraid to look. In the distance, gibbons screeched. It was the barometric shift in the air.

They knew something was wrong.

They knew what was coming.

"It's okay," Elliot repeated, his lips dry and bloodless.

But he was still catching his breath when his phone rang.

He checked the caller ID as he slipped his phone from his pocket, hoping it was Emily and frowning when he saw that it wasn't. It was his mom. She'd finally realized he was gone. Elliot's stomach clenched as he let the call go to voice mail, his hand limp on the grass. He leaned his head back, bouncing it gently against the fire engine's tire as he listened to the chug of a nearby generator—ignoring his chirping phone.

All he wanted was to find his sister and bring her home.

They could deal with their mom afterward.

Together.

But the twist in his gut was telling him to stay where he was.

His phone started ringing again almost as soon as his

mom was able to leave a voice mail. Elliot lifted it to his ear slowly, as if he were underwater. Delaying the inevitable. "I'm okay," he said, barely looking up at the firemen as they trudged past him, stepping over his outstretched legs with their heavy boots. One of the firemen looked back quizzically as he ducked into a tent, and Elliot wondered if he had heard his mom yelling on the other end of the line.

Elliot rolled his eyes just in case, to show that he wasn't embarrassed.

"I'm fine," he said. "I just needed to—"

But his mom wasn't listening.

She was on a roll.

"I can't get through to your sister," she screamed, her voice ragged with stress. "And I can't get through to your father, either. I can't get through to anyone. And you're *sick,* Elliot. What are you even thinking?" Elliot pulled a handful of grass from the ground and tossed it into the wind as he waited for her to finish. He hated that she sounded so desperate and he hated that it was his fault. She'd gone through so much already. But Valerie was coming. He could hear the emergency workers preparing while his green confetti swirled ten feet away, caught in invisible updrafts.

Emily was in trouble—they all were, and there was no point denying it.

"Em's out here," he said. "I had to try to find her."

He waited for his mom to say something—*anything*—but there was no answer on the other end of the line.

Just a soft sobbing.

"Mom?"

The two firemen exited the tent, accompanied by the woman named Joy. The firemen were deep in conversation and didn't seem to notice Elliot as they stepped over his legs again. The woman named Joy, on the other hand, knelt next to him—planting her knee in the wet dirt. She typed a quick message on her phone as she waited for him to finish his call. On the other end of the line, Elliot could hear that his mother had placed her own phone on the kitchen counter. He could tell because she was running the sink.

Splashing the tears from her eyes.

He nodded at Joy, his phone still pinned to his ear.

"Hey," she said, looking up from her emails. "You doin' okay?"

Elliot shrugged, his stomach twinging beneath his fingers.

"Yeah," he mumbled. "I can't find my sister, is all."

"Your sister?" Her voice was tight with concern. "She's lost?"

Elliot decided that he liked Joy.

He liked her dirty sneakers and her wrinkled blazer.

And the shirt she was wearing beneath it. A black T-shirt for a band he hadn't heard of. She didn't seem *that* much older than him—not really. It was just the lines around her eyes that made her look like an adult. And the way her lips turned down at their corners. Elliot took his hand away from his stitches to gesture toward the park— where Emily was, *somewhere*—but his shirt was dark and wet where his hand had been.

He clutched his stomach again, hoping she hadn't noticed the blood.

"Where'd you lose her?" she asked, stretching her legs out as she sat next to Elliot and rested her head alongside his on the massive tire. Elliot shifted beside her, making room. The oak leaves rustled overhead, the branches singing in the wind. Joy looked like she could fall asleep then and there. Elliot could recognize the signs—he'd felt the same way every day for the past two weeks—but her phone started ringing almost as soon as she sat down. He could see that she was tempted to ignore it, but even if she wanted to, an older man jogged out from beneath the tent, red-faced and waving his arms.

"Joy," he shouted, his voice thick with a cold. "It's the governor!"

Joy rubbed her eyes as she turned toward Elliot and smiled.

"To be continued," she said, holding up a finger. "Okay?"

Elliot nodded as Joy rolled to her feet, dragging her heels as she paced between the fire trucks, her chopped hair blowing in the wind. The pain had subsided for the most part, but the light-headedness remained. He blinked dizzily up at the gnarled oaks, remembering something his mom had yelled before she'd left her phone on the counter. About the pile of clothes she'd found on Emily's floor, soaking wet and smelling of sewage. Elliot watched Joy circle the tents three times, explaining the NCRC's emergency response strategy to the governor and smiling at Elliot each time she passed him.

When she looped back toward Elliot a fourth time, he was gone.

Like he'd blown away with the coming storm.

AMBERGRIS CAY, ATLANTIC OCEAN

JUNE 11—1:30 P.M.

The petrel floated on a warped plank of sun-whitened wood—once red, now barnacled and worn by the sea. Before it was his life raft, the driftwood had been the uppermost lip of an unnamed fishing boat. That changed in the early hours of the morning, when the swirling vortex of Megastorm Valerie passed overhead, lifting the modest boat a hundred feet above sea level and shattering it against a shallow reef.

What didn't sink to the bottom of the Atlantic Ocean was already washing up on the shores of Port-de-Paix and Baracoa, two hundred miles of rough surf away. The little bird would have washed up with it, drowned and ragged, if the rolling plank hadn't kept his head above the waves.

The petrel blinked.

His eyes were crusted with salt and he hadn't eaten in days.

Below him, the turquoise water was brimming with life.

Neon damselfish darted through swarms of translucent jellies as spiny lobster scuttled across the seafloor, feeding on the detritus of the storm. If he had been able to fly, the little petrel could have eaten his fill.

But he couldn't fly, not yet.

The wind had ripped through his feathers as it spit him into the upper atmosphere, like a rock through a window, and his muscles still burned from fighting the storm. The nightmare had been too much for the little bird to bear, and he'd lost consciousness as he plummeted toward the surf—tossed by the waves of fortune onto the rolling wreckage of the fishing boat.

It was a miracle that he was still alive.

A handful of seagulls wheeled overhead, laughing and chirping as the driftwood raft sloshed over swelling wavelets. The gulls hadn't strayed far from shore. Their home was a small, private island called Ambergris Cay, just thirty short miles north. With the storm well on its way to the southern United States, the sky was clear and blue. If he'd been able to gather his strength, the petrel could have easily made it to the cay's pillow-soft beaches.

If.

The petrel closed his eyes, breathing deeply as parrot-fish chased the tips of his wings, which trailed in the surf behind him. Had he made it just a few more miles through the storm, he would have landed in the Gulf Stream. The warm, oceanic gyre would have ferried him up the eastern seaboard of the United States and across the Atlantic. All the way to Europe and back, as far from Valerie as you could get.

By happenstance, the petrel had crashed into a short-cut instead: a thin equatorial stream cutting all the way to Africa by way of Puerto Rico, four hundred miles away. If he could just keep on breathing, the little petrel would end up exactly where he'd started without having to move a feather.

If he could just keep on breathing . . .

NEW ORLEANS

JUNE 11—2:00 P.M.

The flight to the mainland had been surprisingly smooth, in large part because the second dose of Alejo's painkillers had kicked in somewhere over the Florida Keys. As they approached the sprawling Mississippi River delta, a feeling of warmth and well-being had spread from the pit of his stomach to the tips of his fingers and toes. He'd watched the sky darken over the wetlands and—with the specter of Valerie clawing at their heels—rested his cheek against the double-paned glass.

He'd even surprised himself by falling asleep.

It was only when the plane's wheels hit the crackling asphalt in Venice, Louisiana, that the glowing warmth turned to nausea. Alejo wasn't sure if it was a side effect of the medication or the storm. The airstrip was nothing more than a thin band of weathered blacktop cutting through the wetlands, and the wind screamed across the tall grass that surrounded them, whipping it into waves that pitched and rolled but never crashed.

Alejo had felt seasick just looking at them.

He'd curled down into his seat, his eyes squeezed shut as he waited for the engines to start back up again. For the plane to fly them away from the storm. But the news crew *wasn't* flying away from the storm, like the rest of the still-seated soldiers. They were rushing to meet it in New Orleans, and they were on a tight schedule: Valerie was so close that they had to sprint to outrun her. "Go time, kid," the cameraman had said, tousling his hair as the rest of his crew climbed down to the tarmac. Alejo shielded his face when he joined them, the rain slicing at his good arm as he ran to the nearby helipad, pushing into the wind.

Soaking wet, again.

As soon as he climbed aboard the waiting helicopter, Alejo collapsed, shivering, onto the first empty seat he could find. The pilot had already initiated takeoff, so he strapped himself in as quickly as he could with one arm, then burrowed his head into the crook of his sling and tried to fall back to sleep. *To just get through it.* It should have been an easy trip—a half-hour hop on a good day—but the helicopter had other plans. It twitched and bounced as it cut through the rising jet streams, jerking fitfully into the path of least resistance.

Spinning like a weathervane.

Alejo could feel the vomit rising in his throat.

It burned at the back of his mouth even after the helicopter leveled out, and he didn't dare open his eyes again until they began their descent into the city of New Orleans. When he finally felt safe enough to sneak a cautious peek at his surroundings, Alejo frowned so deeply that his ears popped from the pressure. The cameraman had inched his way to the very edge of the helicopter's open door, looping his arm through a wall of reinforced nylon webbing so he could lean over the void. A splash of bile crept up past Alejo's molars as the green canopy of a sprawling park rippled and swayed beneath the helicopter's narrow skids.

He swallowed, cringing at the taste.

"It's okay," Alejo whispered, his stomach clenching as he checked the buckle on his seat belt for the third time. The quiver in his voice wasn't reassuring, but he could barely hear himself over the roar of the rotors anyway.

"You're okay," he repeated, taking a deep breath, and then another.

But Alejo wasn't okay.

His wrist had started to throb again—a dull pain pulsing from his palm to his elbow—and his head was swimming. He glanced around the cabin, praying for a quick landing, and accidentally locked eyes with the reporter, who smirked and looked down at his phone. Alejo grit his teeth and forced a smile. He didn't stop smiling until they touched down amid the fire trucks and police cars below them, settling heavily onto the grass.

"Ready?"

The cameraman squeezed Alejo's shoulder, not waiting for a response before he jumped confidently out of the cabin, his heavy boots crunching on twigs blown loose by the helicopter's whirring blades. Alejo gulped. The cameraman's grip had been strong, but not strong enough to reassure Alejo, who stayed buckled into his seat as the cabin emptied.

"C'mon, kid," the cameraman shouted over his shoulder.

Alejo swallowed dryly as he unbuckled his seat belt.

It wasn't easy to do with one hand, but the cameraman waited, checking his battery packs as the rest of the crew made their way through a web of haphazardly parked cars to the makeshift headquarters at their center. When Alejo finally joined him on the ground, the cameraman squatted—making a point of holding his camera at his side as he looked Alejo directly in the eyes. Alejo wanted to look away, to shrug his shoulders and climb back into the helicopter—but the cameraman was staring at him so intently that he felt pinned, like a butterfly on a corkboard.

"When we leave . . . ," the cameraman said, his voice rough and low, his breath thick with the stench of cigarettes. "When we leave, we're going to leave running." He spat into the grass, gathering his thoughts as the wind ripped through the green leaves overhead and a siren sounded in the distance.

"So stay close, okay?"

Alejo nodded, but when the cameraman turned to join the rest of the crew beneath a heavy canvas flap, he didn't follow. *He couldn't.* Instead, he stumbled back behind the helicopter, trailing his good hand across the hoods of parked police cruisers until he finally fell to his knees between two fire trucks. His stomach was empty except for a can of diet cola, but it was a minor miracle that he hadn't puked it onto the cameraman's scuffed boots.

That he'd been able to hold it down as long as he had.

Hidden from view, Alejo retched onto the grass.

When he was finished, Alejo wiped the back of his good arm across his chin and headed straight for a water fountain he'd spotted on the far side of the tents. He walked slowly, his feet dragging in the dirt as he ran his tongue across his unbrushed teeth. All around him, people rushed back and forth between matte green tents, gathering in small groups where they talked in hushed voices and strode purposefully across the park, shouting into walkie-talkies. Alejo barely noticed them. All he needed was water, he told himself, to get the taste out of his mouth.

After that, he would be fine.

The stream from the fountain, when he finally reached it, was no more than a trickle. He had to press his lips against the spout to drink, and when he did, the water was hot and metallic. But Alejo drank for a full minute anyway, not stopping until he could feel his empty stomach stretching beneath his shirt. When he was done, he ran the fingers of his good hand across the burbling spout and splashed his cheeks.

"*Está bien*," he said, surveying the park with slightly fresher eyes.

A heavy gust blew through the oaks, kicking up clouds of dust and pollen.

It had been a long day—and it was still only two o'clock in the afternoon. It was hard to believe that he'd been in San Juan just that morning, in the house he shared with Padrino Nando. Watching the waves wash La Perla out to sea. It was different from what Alejo had expected, stateside. He hadn't seen much of the city, it was true. Just a gray and black patchwork of roofs—drab with rain—as they landed . . . and the park. But everything felt so much more spaced out than back home.

So much *emptier.*

Alejo rubbed an itch from his nose as a chorus of leaves sang overhead, joined by the deep baritone of giant wind chimes. He was only a five-minute walk from the tents, but it was so calm and quiet by the water fountain that he felt like he was on another planet. He wondered how far he was from New York City, now that he was in the States. *How far he was from his mother.* For the first time in his life, he couldn't smell the sea—just dirt, wet and rich beneath his feet. Alejo took a deep breath, filling his lungs. If he didn't know what was coming, he would have been tempted to run past the tree line, through the empty park and the maze of streets beyond it.

Instead, he scanned the sky—looking for birds.

"As long as there are birds in the waves," Padrino Nando had said.

Alejo sighed, hoping that the storm hadn't gone too far inland.

That his *padrino* was still safe, wherever he was.

In New Orleans, there wasn't so much as a sparrow in the breeze. And it wasn't just the birds. Not counting the emergency workers, the city had evacuated. Alejo could sense the absence all around him, in the stir of branches overhead and the shouts like whispers in the wind: quiet reminders that he was all alone again, on the precipice of the storm.

All alone except for the boy walking haltingly in the distance.

Alejo straightened, craning his neck as the boy lurched down an embankment toward the overgrown edge of a deep green lagoon. He expected the boy to stop when he reached the shoreline, but he kept going—trudging into the cattails and kicking his legs through the shallows. Alejo frowned as he watched him splash halfway to a small island in the middle of the water. He looked over his shoulder, hoping someone else was watching the boy, too.

That it wasn't just him.

But, except for the boy, Alejo was still alone.

He turned back to the lagoon just in time to see the boy stumble and then fall, clutching his side. "No," Alejo whispered as he disappeared beneath the glassy green water, but the lagoon was far enough away that he second-guessed what he had seen. The boy could have spotted something—a coin or a ring, the silver glint of metal in the mud. *Anything*. For a split second, Alejo stood motionless, not realizing that he was holding his breath.

Waiting for the boy to resurface.

As the ripples in the water began to fade, Alejo jumped into action.

"Hey!" he shouted, but there was nobody around to hear him. He pivoted toward the camp, looking for someone—for *anyone*—who could help. In the distance, he spotted police officers and firefighters milling around their vehicles, biding time until they were deployed. But the water fountain was so far away. Too far away for them to hear Alejo over the rising wind and too far away for Alejo to run back to the tents for help.

He didn't have a choice.

His heart pounded as he sprinted toward the water.

"Hey!" Alejo shouted again, yelling at the top of his lungs.

Hoping his voice would carry.

"Help!"

A girl emerged—horror-struck—from the island's shaggy brush as Alejo ripped his sling off, tossing it behind him as he ran. His swollen hand hung limply from his arm. It hurt worse and worse with every footfall, but the oversized sling slowed him down and there wasn't any time to waste. The girl crashed through the tall grass, diving into the dark lagoon headfirst while Alejo splashed into the cold, wet muck. It was softer than he expected and it pulled at his shoes, tripping him into the water. Slowing him down to a sputtering stumble. By the time he reached the drowning boy, the girl was already struggling to keep his head above water.

Their faces were both spangled with duckweed.

Alejo's was too.

He could feel it sticking in his hair and ears—tiny green clovers with long, wet roots. A goose honked from shore as Alejo stood in the waist-deep lagoon, dripping wet and thrusting both of his hands, good and bad, beneath the boy's armpits. He tried to ignore the pain as he lifted, straining to drag the boy's limp body from the water—but his wrist wouldn't let him. He swore that he could feel a broken bone clicking in his arm and yelled, unable to contain himself.

Still, nobody heard him.

Nobody except the girl and the goose, who shuffled nervously back and forth on the shore, honking imperiously as the girl helped Alejo pull the boy into the reeds. The sky opened up almost as soon as he stepped out of the water, the rain hard enough to sting, but the girl didn't follow him to shore. Instead, she stood in the downpour, shivering with shock, like she'd seen a ghost.

But the boy was still alive.

Even before he coughed himself awake, Alejo could see that. The bent reeds beneath him were smeared with blood, but the boy's chest rose and fell gently beneath the trees while the sky shattered with lightning. The girl ran to the boy's side as dirty water dripped down his chin, into the collar of his wrinkled shirt. She whispered his name over and over again, her voice lost beneath the rolling thunder. "You're not supposed to be here," she mumbled, her tears streaking the mud on her face as she cradled his head in her arms.

Alejo stepped toward the girl, to help her somehow, but the goose nipped protectively at his bare legs—chasing him back into deeper water. *"Basta,"* Alejo said, falling back into the mud. He blinked the rain from his eyes as the goose charged toward him, its chest puffed out to twice its normal size. "Stop it!" Alejo shouted, waving his good hand at the angry bird.

Startling the girl.

She looked up at Alejo as if she'd just noticed he was there.

"It's okay," she said, more to the goose than to Alejo.

The goose waddled happily toward the girl's gentle voice, nuzzling its head against her outstretched hand as another bolt of lightning split the sky. It struck so close that Alejo could smell its sizzle. He jumped back to land as a crack of thunder rolled and rumbled through the darkening clouds. The thunder echoed across the empty city, heralding rain so heavy it came down in sheets and buckets. As if on cue, Alejo and the girl rushed to drag the boy farther ashore, pulling him through the reeds and the mud to a dense outcropping of trees. They propped him against a knotted trunk, beneath a layer of leaves so thick that even the megastorm couldn't break through.

It hadn't yet, anyway.

Sheltered by the twisted limbs and cocooned in a thick curtain of rain, the helicopter and the news crew might as well have been a thousand miles away. Alejo joined the girl, who was sitting cross-legged next to the boy, looking at his wound but not touching it. It was bad enough that he would need a doctor—that much was obvious. His shirt was stained with blood, and it had been hard enough getting him out of the lagoon. If they didn't want him to drown again, they'd need more help to get him off the island.

"Is he okay?" Alejo asked.

The girl shook her head.

Her face was streaked with grime and tears, and as the storm raged around them, Alejo wondered who she was and how long she'd been camping there. Her hair was wet and plastered to her neck, and algae from the lagoon clung to her arms and legs. The goose settled down next to the girl, eyeing him suspiciously as it tucked its beak beneath its mangled wing. Alejo cradled his own hurt wing in his good arm as he balanced on a knobby root, staring at the girl and the boy and the goose.

Wondering what to do next.

"He's my brother," the girl said, not looking up. "Elliot. That's his name."

She rubbed her nose with the back of her hand, then wiped her hand on the goose.

"He's sick. He can't be around germs or leave his room or . . ."

She trailed off and Alejo didn't fill the silence.

His wrist, squeezed tightly into the warmth of his armpit, was throbbing—and the boy, Elliot, had started coughing again. Alejo watched him as he groaned back into consciousness, clutching at his stomach and doubling over into the dirt. It was painful to watch, and Alejo stepped toward the wall of rain, preparing to brave the lightning and the lagoon—to sprint back to the tents for help—when Elliot finally opened his eyes.

He looked up at Alejo and then at his sister and smiled.

"Emily," he said. "I found you."

His voice was little more than a rasp, and his lips were cracked and spackled in algae. But he was awake and he was smiling. Emily frowned through her tears, then smiled through her frown. Alejo couldn't help but smile, too. As the girl hugged her brother, the first drops of Megastorm Valerie broke through the thick canopy above their heads—funneling down between the cracks in the layers of leaves, dripping into the soil beneath their feet. Compared to the storm beyond the muddy shores, it was barely a drizzle. For the moment, they were high and dry . . .

But that moment was quickly passing.

TENT CITY

"*C'mon*," Silas said, tapping his heavy boot against the gas.

The drive to New Orleans had taken twice as long as it should have. There was flooding in Belle Chasse—bad enough that half the roads were out—and so little visibility on the bridge that Silas had crossed it blind, slowing to a crawl to keep from crashing into the river. Every few minutes, the radio buzzed with an emergency broadcast. Silas had still been plowing through puddles on LA-23 when the first one broke through the static. He'd gripped the steering wheel, cursing under his breath as city officials announced a mandatory evacuation. Expecting gridlock, they'd reversed the flow of traffic on all south-bound highways, sealing the city off before the storm.

Silas prayed that Sarah had fixed things up with their daughter.

That they hadn't waited for him and were already on the road.

But he had no way to find out.

His phone didn't have any reception, and he'd thrown it to the floor the last time he'd tried and failed to reach them. It slid beneath the passenger seat while Silas raced home, scanning the radio for the hundredth time. Searching for a clear signal in the deserted city, for someone to tell him that he wasn't too late. But all Silas could find was country music. The plaintive cry of steel guitars joined the drumming rain as he sped through familiar streets, not bothering to slow down for stop signs or red lights. Half hoping, as he turned onto his block, that their apartment would be empty.

And half hoping to see his wife and kids.

To save them from the storm.

Either way, Silas had no idea what to expect until he slammed on his brakes, his rear wheels skidding on the asphalt as his wife stared at him from the middle of the road. White-faced, her outstretched hands pressed against the hood of his oversized truck. Silas threw the door open, blocking the empty road and jumping into the rain—the country music following him onto the street as he rushed to meet his wife. "Sarah," he shouted, pulling her into his arms. "Let's get the kids, come on, let's go!"

But something wasn't right.

Sarah was shaking.

She was crying.

"They're gone," she said. "They're both gone."

"They're what?" Silas asked, swallowing a mounting dread. "It's okay," he said, filling in the blanks when his wife refused to answer. "Wherever they are, we have time, Sarah—we can pick them up. We just need to go, okay?"

"You don't understand," she whispered, pushing Silas away, her fists clenching helplessly in the rain. "I don't know where they are and they're not answering their phones."

Silas held his wife tighter as he tried to process what she was telling him.

Megastorm Valerie was bearing down on them, and their kids—their sick little boy and their baby girl—were missing. He should have been worried. He should have panicked. Any person in their right mind would have. But Silas couldn't let himself panic, not with so much on the line. He was used to emergencies, he told himself. They happened all the time on the rig, and the only way to get through them was to *think* through them, one step at a time. He pressed his lips against the top of Sarah's head, tasting the rain in her hair as he tried to think past the adrenaline coursing through his veins.

Their apartment was too small to hide in and there was nowhere else to go.

Not now that the city was shut down.

Silas frowned.

The streetcars had stopped running, and the only place he could think of—within walking distance—was ground zero: the emergency headquarters he'd heard about on the radio. Everywhere else had been evacuated, and the park was just a few blocks away. Their kids would have heard the helicopters and fire engines. He didn't like it, but with nothing else to do, Silas could see them being drawn to the excitement.

"It's okay," he said, hugging his shivering wife in the rain.

Hoping he was right.

"We've got this, okay?"

—

Silas walked quickly, jogging to keep up with his wife so he could stretch a wide blue tarp over her head as well as his own. Not that it was doing much good. The cuffs of his jeans were thick with mud and the tarp pooled and overflowed as he chased after her, the rain stinging his fingers. It was coming down so hard that he had to shout to be heard over it, but Sarah didn't seem to mind the downpour, or even notice it.

If his wife was anything, she was resilient.

She'd had to be, with everything she'd gone through this past year.

It hadn't been five minutes since Silas found her on the street in front of their apartment, and as she stepped onto the wet grass in front of the makeshift camp, he watched her transform into a woman on a mission. Soaking wet and full of fight, she darted from tent to tent—lifting the flaps and peeking inside, calling for their kids.

Calling for Emily.

Silas was glad that she'd found her second wind, because he'd started to second-guess himself as the storm gained strength. It was as if the entire city was stuck between radio stations, trapped in a static hiss, and the rain was so thick that he could barely make out his own hands when he held them two feet from his face. Assuming he was right about Emily and Elliot—assuming they were in the park somewhere—they had three hundred fifty acres to search before Valerie came crashing down on them.

"Emily!"

Sarah's voice hit a ragged upper register as she ran to the next empty tent, and then the next. Silas caught up with her long enough to wrap his arm around her shoulder. To pull her into a protective hug beneath the tarp.

"I'm sure they're around here somewhere," he said.

But he didn't *feel* sure.

Not anymore.

He couldn't imagine his kids staying outside in this weather, and Sarah was running out of tents to check. Meanwhile, what Silas *could* see of the camp was turning into a ghost town before his eyes. Pre-responders in plastic ponchos darted through the deluge to their cars, gouging huge tracks in the grass as they peeled out of the park. They weren't going to be any use to anyone drowned—and with Valerie's foot on the gas, they were running out of time.

Silas blinked the water from his eyes, then closed them.

He wished he'd left the rig earlier.

That he'd driven through the night.

Even with the slap of the rain against the tarp, he could hear the storm more than he could see it. There was a vibration in the air—and in the ground. Something separate from the sudden onslaught of thunder and lightning. It reminded Silas of the distant grind of a five-hundred-pound drill bit into the seafloor beneath P7 Beta. Of the way you could *feel* it, just barely, through the soles of your boots. He pricked his ears, his brow furrowing as he let the tarp drop to the ground. The rain stung his forehead and cheeks, running down his neck and chest and into his jeans, which sagged on his waist as they soaked up the storm. It was only when he opened his eyes—blinking into the rain—that it truly hit him. . . .

The vibration, the seismic waves.

It was like an earthquake.

In that moment, as Valerie beat down onto his upturned face, Silas imagined Valerie screaming through the Gulf with waves so violent they ripped the rig from its moorings. So strong they made the ground shake a hundred miles away. There were over two thousand deep-sea rigs off the coast of Louisiana, and Silas could almost hear their metal twisting in the wind—rusted screws popping like bullets in the swirling vortex of the storm.

Silas held his breath, hoping he was wrong.

But as much as he hated to admit it, he could feel the ground buzzing—barely perceptibly—beneath his boots, with the steady rhythm of crashing waves. As Sarah trembled at the entrance of the last tent, Silas prayed for a miracle. For Emily and Elliot to be hiding behind the flaps, safe and dry. For his family to make it through to the other side of the storm, somehow.

"Emily," Sarah whispered, trailing off as her face crumpled into a silent sob.

"Elliot . . ."

—

Joy Harrison looked up from her computer, annoyed and running on zero hours of sleep, as Silas joined his wife at the flap. Unlike the tents they'd already checked, the last tent was full of people. But none of them were children. Joy turned back to her computer, scrolling through updated warnings as the rest of the NCRC curled up on fold-up cots, laid out by a particularly virulent strain of seasonal flu.

The thunder overhead was never-ending, a constant rumble punctuated by the occasional spine-shivering shock of lightning. Valerie was ahead of schedule—so far ahead that even the NCRC had been taken by surprise. That is, the last remaining member of the NCRC still well enough to read the signs. Almost as soon as it started raining, Joy had double-checked her monitor and given orders to disband the encampment, citing a massive cloudbank that dwarfed the skyline. Local disaster response teams began evacuating soon afterward, and FEMA was right behind them. The only boots still on the ground were Joy's dirty white Converse, and they were drenched through to her socks.

"Update on landfall?" she asked, tapping her headset.

"And are the highways clear?"

She gestured for Silas and Sarah to enter, then abruptly stood, striding across the length of the tent as she waited for a response. The rain had come so fast and hard that it had crept beneath the waxed canvas edges, so much so that the ground was soggy beneath her feet.

Not a good sign.

"Okay," Joy said, but she hadn't gotten the answer she'd been hoping for.

For the storm to have come this quickly—four hours ahead of an already expedited schedule—meant two things: (1) the storm was stronger and faster than they predicted, and (2) they had less time than they expected to evacuate. In fact, according to the latest readings, they should have been gone an hour ago. Lives were on the line, and Dr. Abigail Carson and the rest of the team were too sick to be any help. Only Rob—their data analyst— was halfway well enough to be useful, and he was a computer guy. Not the action hero Joy would have chosen to send out into a BDD, but desperate times called for desperate measures.

"Rob," Joy said, kicking the foot of his cot with the toe of her sneaker.

Rob sat up slowly, sniffling as he rubbed the crust from his eyes.

"Help these people find their kids, okay?"

He wasn't much of a search party, but Joy had seen the boy earlier and knew he was lurking around the tents. Besides, she had the rest of the city to worry about. By the time Rob stood up, she was already fielding another call on her headset. But Silas didn't leave—not even after Rob pulled on his shoes. He waited, his wife pulling anxiously on his arm, until Joy was done barking orders; then he told her about what he'd felt.

What he was *still* feeling—the vibrations beneath their feet.

"You're with the NCRC," he said. "You see stuff like this all the time, right?"

Joy stared at Silas for long moment.

She was overworked and exhausted, and she wished she could say that Silas was imagining things. The truth was, the tremors he was describing weren't news to her. They hadn't been on any of the NCRC's earlier projections, but as soon as they started registering, she'd been inundated with seismographic readings from their home base in Washington, DC.

She just hadn't known what to do with them.

Nobody did.

They were a complete anomaly.

Valerie was a complete anomaly.

"So," Silas asked. "What's the protocol here?"

He stole a quick glance at the various monitors peppered throughout the tent. There were graphs on most of the monitors—black lines that spiked into an alarming shade of red. The specifics of the data may have been nuanced, but the general idea wasn't difficult to understand.

"You guys have some special emergency plan, right?" Joy shook her head.

"We get as many people as we can as far away as possible," she said, turning back to her computer. "Preferably before the storm hits."

The tent went silent except for the pounding rush of rain and Joy's clicking keyboard—but Silas didn't have time for follow-up questions. His kids were out there somewhere, in the storm, and there was no one to call—no cavalry coming to save them. He folded his calloused hand around his wife's trembling fingers and nodded at Rob.

"We're not leaving without our kids," he said.

Rob frowned as he followed them back out into the storm, unsure of what to say.

"Rob," Joy called after him. "Ten minutes, max."

FEATHER ISLAND

"I was going to bring you out here," Emily said, nervously tapping the mud-streaked cover of her book. "I was just planning to wait until you were better, is all." Elliot sighed, clutching his stomach as he stared up into the dripping canopy. He wasn't sure if his stitches had stopped bleeding, but the wound still stung enough to take his breath away and he didn't have the courage to check. Meanwhile, the new kid paced beneath the trees, circling the still mostly dry interior of the tiny island.

Taking stock.

There wasn't much to see.

A heavy veil of rain surrounded them on all sides, so

thick that it was impossible to make out the rest of the park. There were enough shaggy trees on the island to shelter them, at least for a little while longer, but the rain had started to crack through the upper branches and a sogginess was spreading from the edges of the island inward. Fresh mud mixed with feathers left by the ducks and geese that roosted there alongside herons and more exotic birds. Except for Emily's little friend, most of them had flown away long before the rain had even started.

Emily wished she could fly away, too, but she wasn't sure what to do about Elliot.

He wasn't looking good, and she couldn't ignore it any longer.

They had to do something.

She had to do something.

"Hey," Emily said, joining the new kid at the edge of the tree line. The rain was hitting the dirt so hard that it splashed back against her shins, splattering them with mud. The new kid was getting splashed, too, but he wasn't jumping back beneath the trees, so Emily didn't either. "I don't think I could have gotten him out of there without you," she said. "That was awesome."

The new kid didn't answer.

He just stared into the storm.

"I was thinking that we can wait for this to let up," she

said, nodding toward the white-hot bursts of lightning in the darkening sky. "Then we can make a run for it."

"It's not *going* to let up," he said.

Emily frowned as the new kid rubbed goose bumps from his arm.

"The storm, it's *la tormenta del siglo*—the storm of the century."

The new kid turned to Emily, squinting through the rain. He was skinnier than Emily and seemed younger than her, too, but there was something about his pained smile that made her feel like she was five years old. "It's going to keep coming and coming," he said, holding his left hand out for an awkward handshake. For the first time since they reached the island, Emily noticed that his other wrist was hanging limply at his side.

Hurt.

She clutched her book beneath her armpit and shook his outstretched hand.

It was small and slick with rain, but warm and strong.

"My name's Alejo," he said. "I came here with the news crew, in a helicopter."

"I'm Emily," Emily said. "And this is Elliot."

Elliot didn't respond except to bounce his head against the soft bark as he stared up into the trees, delirious with pain. Noticing that his phone had slipped from the loose pockets of his basketball shorts, Emily kneeled beside him and wiped the dirt and duckweed from its screen. It was wet from his fall, but it was still working—*sort of.*

Alejo leaned in close, watching as Emily tried to make a call. . . .

But she didn't even get a busy signal.

Just dead air.

"The storm of the *century*?" Emily asked.

Alejo nodded.

They were running out of options, and Alejo didn't look like he was going to be much help. Emily tried not to stare, but now that she knew he was hurt, she couldn't stop herself. His bad wrist looked like a ripe plum—so swollen that he was having trouble moving it—and she could tell from the way he grimaced that it was getting worse. They'd only barely made it onto the island with his help; without it, she wasn't sure that they'd be able to leave.

Not with Elliot, anyway.

"We could try to stay here," she suggested, jumping up to inspect the perimeter. Her sneakers slid in the wet grass, which was only growing wetter with every passing minute. But there were still dry spots, both on the ground and in the forked and folding branches overhead.

They could improvise.

Emily put on a brave face.

"It'll be like in *My Side of the Mountain*," she said.

"That's just a book," Elliot groaned, bumping the back of his head against the trunk for emphasis. Loose bark crumbled onto his shoulders, and Emily's turtle poked his nose out from her backpack to investigate. He crawled halfway into Elliot's lap, snapping happily at the mossy bits—oblivious to the mounting storm. Elliot's eyes widened as he stared down at the turtle and then back at his sister.

Torn between laughter and despair.

He stroked the turtle's head with the tip of his finger as Emily looked to Alejo for support. But Alejo was squatting in the mud, inspecting a shallow puddle. "Hey," she said, crouching next to him as he held his good hand just above its surface—watching the water shimmer in the wind. Emily cocked her head as she stared into her own rippling reflection.

There was something about it that looked wrong to her somehow.

Something she couldn't quite explain.

"What is it?" Emily asked, watching the corners of Alejo's mouth twitch in horror as the puddle danced beneath his palm. Elliot stopped bouncing his head against the tree and sat up straight, his face pale with effort.

"What's going on?" he asked, but Alejo didn't answer. Instead, he held Emily's hand above the muddy water so she could feel it, too. Elliot shifted, leaning forward for a better view—but there was nothing to see. Just the look of consternation on Emily's face as the puddle jumped to meet her fingers.

"You feel it coming," Alejo whispered. "Right?"

Whatever it was, it was like the pounding of a distant drum.

Her palm shook over the dancing water as the turtle retreated into the safety of her backpack, sensing danger. Something terrible was happening and they needed to leave, to get as far away from the storm as possible. But Emily was too scared to think, and before she could even *start* to formulate a plan, lightning struck a nearby tree—close enough that she could smell it burning, even in the rain.

Emily screamed.

She couldn't help herself.

The lightning touched down like an explosion, so loudly that her own shrieks sounded muted in her ears—like they were coming from someone else. From *somewhere* else. Thunder cracked and tumbled overhead as Emily jumped deeper beneath the cover of the tiny island, running toward her brother and away from the rain.

Alejo wasn't far behind.

"We're not safe here," he said.

Emily nodded, not trusting her voice not to catch in her throat.

She stood speechless, watching as Elliot loosened his grip on his side—testing to see if the bleeding had stopped. It hadn't. Emily and Alejo shared a worried look as they watched a darkness spreading through his shirt, between his dirty fingers. Emily swallowed, swinging her backpack to her shoulders as Elliot closed his eyes and rolled his head against the tree.

"You two stay here," she said. "I'm going for help."

Emily turned on her heels, running to the edge of the island before Alejo could try to stop her. Before she could stop herself. She was already leaning into the wind and the rain, her feet settling into the deeper mud of the flooding banks, when she felt Alejo's good hand on her shoulder.

"I'm coming, too," he shouted.

"He can't be alone," Emily said. "And it's up to me—"

"To save him?" Alejo shook his head. "What if *you* need help?" he asked.

Emily thought it over.

She didn't have time to argue.

The faster they were able to get Elliot to safety, the

better, and Alejo had already helped her once today. Wounded wrist and all. The rain was fast and hard and stung their faces as they stepped through the bramble and into the knee-deep water, but they kept walking— tripping through the mud into the lagoon; stumbling and falling as the thunder shook more rain loose from the sky. In their wake, the last able-bodied birds in Audubon Park erupted from the upper branches of the island. Shaken from their perches, a plague of oil-feathered grackles arced high over the battered canopy—coasting upward through the downpour on warm, northbound currents.

Leaving their nests behind.

Distant voices broke through the rain.

In her excitement, Emily slipped in the mud.

"Help!" she yelled, splashing awkwardly to shore. "Someone's hurt!"

They were halfway there, just thirty feet from land, but she couldn't see the men who were calling through the storm. The rain was too thick and too unrelenting, and the muck beneath their feet trembled, like Jell-O on a train track—*vibrating*. Alejo steadied his bad arm on her shoulder as Emily covered her eyes, squinting as a spotlight swept back and forth across her face. Zeroing in on their position.

"Hey!" Emily shouted, waving into the blinding light.

She fell to her knees as the ground shook beneath their feet.

"Help us!"

——

The grackles didn't get very far before they alighted, perching beneath gutters and in the eaves of dormer windows as they tried to make sense of the storm. Five blocks away from the tiny island, a well-fed juvenile preened on the sill outside Emily's living room, attempting to shake its feathers dry as the television played to an empty couch. The apartment was similarly empty, even though the front door was ajar and bouncing on its hinges. The lights flickered on and off as the first waves of Megastorm Valerie drenched the little bird. The building wouldn't have electricity much longer, but for now, Emily and Alejo waved from the television screen, live on Channel 4 news.

To the young grackle, they were just two grainy black spots on the dry side of the window, shadows in the noise of the storm. It dug its claws into the soft wood of the windowsill, anchoring itself against the wind while the reporter shouted from the television. The white-hot lights of the news crew illuminated the reporter's dripping face as the image jumped out of focus and then steadied, refocusing on a trembling blade of grass. The cameraman had set his camera on the ground and sprinted toward the island, abandoning the broadcast. He was just barely visible in the corner of the frame, diving into the shallow water.

"We seem to be having a technical difficulty," the reporter announced, trying to sound like he was in control of the situation. His wet shoes filled the screen as he gestured for someone to pick up the camera. They were made from a thin Italian leather, too fancy for the weather. "Hey," the reporter yelled, chasing after the cameraman. *"This is a live feed, genius."*

Just as the reporter began to swear, the broadcast cut to a commercial.

It didn't matter.

The television in Emily's apartment had gone dark.

An electrical transformer had exploded two blocks from the park—the first of many. They sparked blue, then green and orange and pink, flaring out like fireworks atop crooked telephone poles.

Somewhere below the empty apartment, a window shattered.

The wind whistled and howled as it blew across the broken pane, a lonely flourish to announce the approaching storm. Startled, the ruffled grackle took flight—its little beak open, panting as it launched itself upward into the rippling currents. Elsewhere in the abandoned city, car alarms shrieked and wailed, triggered by small seismic tremors that shivered up through rubber wheels and into windshields.

Shaking hairline fractures into the glass.

NCRC

Nobody had been in the offices of the National Climatic Research Center for at least twelve hours, but the bank of monitors above Joy's desk continued to update with projections of the storm. Red lights flashed with each new model, alerting the empty room to storm surges that could reach the northern prairies of Missouri and seismic tremors fissuring the soft sediment of the Mississippi delta. In the entire fifty-year history of the NCRC, the potential for destruction was unprecedented.

And it was only getting worse.

As Megastorm Valerie shifted her bulk from the Gulf of Mexico onto the shuddering shores of the southern United States, the emergency lights flickered and died, enveloping the office in darkness. There wasn't anybody in the room to witness the monitors fade to black, and even if there had been, there was nothing they could have done about it.

Valerie was out of their control.

For the first few seconds after landfall, the outage was localized to New Orleans, but as transformers popped and fizzled, the blackout quickly cascaded into Alabama and South Carolina, overloading power stations and substations all the way up the eastern seaboard. Satellite images showed the darkness climbing up the coast like a time-lapse video of mold in a petri dish.

Satellite images that the NCRC couldn't access.

Not without power.

An automated generator switched on in the basement of the sprawling government building. It hummed underfoot, reverberating through the tile floors as fluorescent lights crackled to life overhead. One by one, the NCRC workstations booted up. Except for Joy's personal laptop, they all defaulted to password-protected log-in screens. Joy's computer, on the other hand, started playing where she'd paused it. A reedy voice from a black-and-white monster movie shouted into the empty room.

"Hey, what are you doing out there—come back!"

The warning lights started flashing again as a webbed creature crept through the deep water of her smudged screen, stalking the silhouette of a swimming woman. The soundtrack swelled ominously from Joy's tiny speakers, reaching a crescendo as a phone began to ring in Dr. Abigail Carson's office. With no one in the room to answer it, the phone rang and rang as a boat full of explorers chased after the monster, readying their nets and harpoons.

Finally, the caller gave up and left a voice mail.

"Dr. Carson," a man said.

He sounded distracted.

"Dr. Carson, this is the president's office." There was shouting in the room behind him, and he muffled the phone with his hand as the explorers continued to hunt the Creature from the Black Lagoon on Joy's laptop. "The president was watching the news when the power went out," the man finally said.

He paused for a breath as another argument broke out in the background.

"Abby, she needs to know how bad this thing really is."

AUDUBON PARK

NEW ORLEANS

JUNE 11—3:15 P.M.

Elliot stared listlessly into the canopy, blinking the rain out of his eyes as it dripped down through the leaves and onto his upturned face. He clutched his side, applying pressure to his wound even though it didn't seem to help. Not really. His stomach throbbed beneath his dirty fingers, so badly that he wanted to check it again—to see just how broken he really was. But he couldn't make himself look.

He didn't want to see the blood . . . he couldn't handle it.

But he half smiled at the irony.

He'd switched places with his little sister.

It was Emily's turn to save *him* now.

274

The megastorm was so close he could feel it in his bones. Tiny ripples pulsed through every puddle on the island, the vibrations spreading outward and up through his outstretched legs. With his nonclutching hand, Elliot reached into the pocket of his shorts, remembering the big blue pills he'd palmed for later. He didn't care that they made him tired—he'd held off as long as he could, and he needed to manage the pain before it got even worse.

Worse.

Elliot smirked at the thought.

He was trapped and bleeding on a tiny island in the middle of a megastorm.

It was hard to imagine his situation getting any worse.

But the medicine was gone.

Elliot squeezed his eyes shut in frustration as he felt through the leaves at his side with the tips of his fingers, digging until he connected with the smooth surface of his missing pills. He popped them into his mouth as soon as he found them—without looking, before he had a chance to lose them again—and tasted grit as he swallowed. Elliot rolled the dirt around on his tongue, spitting as lightning splintered the sky overhead. He hoped his sister would be back soon with help. She'd only been gone a few minutes, but the storm was coming in hard and fast.

If she took much longer, he'd have to try to make it across the lagoon on his own.

It hurt to even think about.

A twig crunched, and Elliot's eyes snapped open—but it wasn't his sister or her new friend. Just a plump goose who'd decided to join him at the base of his tree.

"Don't worry," Elliot said out loud, addressing the goose. "She's coming."

The goose blinked twice, shuffling nervously around Elliot's feet.

He couldn't help but laugh when it stepped onto his lap, honking mournfully as it tucked its broken wing against its breast and settled down. The goose was one of Audubon Park's regulars, so used to people feeding it that it expected special attention. Elliot didn't mind. "Everyone left you, too, huh?" he said, resting his hand on the bird's back as its soft undercarriage warmed his legs. If he tried, Elliot could almost pretend that he was home in bed, tucked beneath his blankets with a pile of unread comics at his side. He yawned, which meant the medicine was kicking in. It wasn't until he heard footsteps crashing through the brush that he opened his eyes again.

"Hey," he mumbled sleepily, expecting his sister.

But it wasn't his sister.

Not even close.

The goose hissed as a man with a scraggly beard jogged toward them in jeans wet up to his thighs. He was wearing a utility vest covered in Velcro strips and pouches bulging with camera lenses. "Sorry," the man said, pushing the goose out of Elliot's lap. He squatted and the goose nipped at his heels, but he ignored the attack as he folded Elliot into his arms and grunted—the veins and muscles in his neck straining from the effort as he stood back up again.

Elliot couldn't think of anything to say, so he didn't say anything.

He just let himself be rescued.

Cattails slapped his face and legs as the bearded man splashed through the reeds surrounding the tiny island, ferrying Elliot to the mainland. He could feel the soft floor of the lagoon trembling ominously beneath the man's boots, but as they neared the far shore, he was reassured by the sounds of his sister shouting and splashing into the water to meet him. Elliot blinked through the rain, recognizing the bright lights of a news crew behind her.

As thankful as he was to be off the island, he hoped they weren't there for him.

It felt so stupid to be saved like this.

Carried like a baby.

Elliot peered into the storm.

The bright lights seemed to be moving, like lanterns swaying on a foggy bridge—swaying . . . and falling to the ground as the grass rolled beneath them. Elliot tightened his hold around the bearded man's neck, watching in horror as the lights sparked into darkness while trees shook on the horizon. The bearded man cursed, planting his legs into the thick mud to ride out the tremor while the rest of the news crew dropped their equipment and sprinted into the piercing rain.

Leaving Emily and the new kid alone in the shallows.

—

Alejo was ankle deep in the lagoon when the first of the major tremors shook their way through the park. He could feel them working their way up his legs, his knees turning to jelly as he stumbled backward into the mud. It was like stepping off a runaway skateboard . . . but still rolling. Unable to fall and unable to stand without falling. Emily splashed wildly at his side, clutching his hand to steady herself as she flailed through the aftershocks.

His bad hand.

Alejo screamed as his swollen wrist clicked against her palm.

The cameraman—halfway across the lagoon with Elliot in his arms—stared, openmouthed. Elliot stared, too. But not at Alejo, whose eyes were watering, his tears mixing with the unrelenting rain. Cradling his arm against his soaking chest, Alejo turned in time to see the rest of the news crew sprinting for the helicopter that was waiting for them beyond the tents.

Abandoning Alejo and his friends.

Alejo shouted.

Not to stop them, but to warn them.

"Watch out!" he yelled, his voice lost in the wind.

It was hard to know what else to say.

If they had just looked before they scattered, they would have seen the tent filling with wind and straining against its stakes. They would have stopped in their tracks as it fought the storm and failed, mushrooming up beneath the clouds. The reporter with the slick shoes was the first to notice, pivoting away from the makeshift camp as the tent burst free from its moorings and spun wildly overhead. Its heavy canvas straps whistled through the wind like sharpened knives as he changed course, ducking down into a black government SUV. The rest of the crew wasn't far behind. They flocked like crows: black shadows against the horizon, pumping their arms as they ran—desperate to get away as fast as they could.

Desperate to save themselves.

By the time the cameraman finally reached shore,

staggering under the weight of the boy in his arms, the SUV was already fishtailing through the mud—halfway out of the park. "Run!" the cameraman shouted, pointing toward the helicopter with his scraggly chin. The tent swirled and spun above their heads as they raced through the storm, shielding their eyes and hoping for the best.

They didn't have a choice.

The rest of the camp had already evacuated, and the helicopter was their only ticket out. "Last chance," the cameraman yelled as they hustled through the billowing tents. Alejo joined in, shouting at the top of his lungs—not even making words, just howling as he sprinted toward the empty field where the cars had parked. There was only one person left in the NCRC's satellite headquarters—only one person who heard them as they screamed their way to safety. Her short hair whipped in the wind when she stepped out from beneath a flap, her eyes widening at the sight of the abandoned camp. She held her walkie-talkie to her mouth as she ran alongside Alejo, barking orders into the receiver as they splashed into the grass. The lawn had turned to mud, and the mud was so gouged by tires that the tread marks had filled with rain, forming puddles.

The puddles rippled underfoot as Alejo climbed aboard the helicopter, helping Emily up behind him.

Breathless from the sprint, he strapped in to his old seat, snapping the buckle shut with this good hand like he'd been doing it his entire life. The cameraman set Elliot down next to him as the woman flipped through the channels on her walkie-talkie, trying to find a frequency strong enough to cut through the noise of the storm. Alejo watched her chew her bright blue fingernails as she paced back and forth across the tiny cabin, the walkie-talkie spitting static in her hand.

"Go time," the cameraman shouted, scrambling into the front seat next to the waiting pilot. "Everyone else is over and out," he said, pointing at the fading red taillights of the SUV on the avenue. The pilot nodded and reached for a switch on the ceiling, initiating takeoff. The rotor started spinning, slowly—wobbling as it worked against the wind.

"Wait," the woman with the walkie-talkie said. "I *know* this kid."

The cameraman twisted in his seat, looking back into the cabin.

Emily's eyes narrowed as she looked from the woman to Elliot and back.

"His parents," she said. "I think they're still out there."

Alejo could feel Emily stiffen next to him.

His parents were her parents, too.

"Oh my God," she whispered, pulling at her seat belt.

Her fingers fumbled as she unbuckled the clasp that was holding her down. Everything had happened too fast. She'd been so swept up in their own escape—so frightened for her injured brother—that it hadn't occurred to her to worry about the rest of her family, too. For once, Alejo was thankful that his own mother was so far away, but he couldn't help thinking about Padrino Nando.

He was out there, too, somewhere.

Alejo hoped he'd made it to safety. . . .

That he wasn't lost in the storm, like Emily's parents.

The adrenaline pumping through Alejo's veins chilled at the thought of it.

"We don't have time," the pilot shouted, pulling at the cameraman's sleeves—trying to stop him as he clambered out of the copilot's chair and jumped into the storm. The pilot glared—red-faced—in the rearview mirror as the cameraman jogged back into the park, shouting for stragglers. "He gets two minutes," the pilot announced, brusquely and to no one in particular. A fresh downpour strafed the windshield and he squinted through it, trying to keep track of the cameraman as he disappeared into one tent and then another.

"Two minutes and we're gone," he mumbled.

Alejo's knees bobbed uncontrollably, toes tapping

the metal grating beneath his feet as the seconds ticked away. Elliot was half asleep, drooling against his shoulder straps, and Emily looked anxious. Like she was planning to jump out of the helicopter, too. Alejo unbuckled his seat belt, just in case she did. He didn't want to go out into the storm again, but if it came down to it, he would help her look.

With more eyes, they could find her parents faster.

And when they did, they could leave this place behind.

As Alejo bounced nervously in his seat, the woman squeezed past him and climbed into the cockpit—taking the cameraman's place in the copilot's chair. She propped her walkie-talkie on the dashboard as she settled down next to the frowning pilot, speaking softly as she gestured toward the empty field. The storm echoed through the cabin as the rain slashed against the helicopter, so hard that Alejo had to strain to hear her.

"We need more eyes on the ground," she said. "That's an order."

Alejo watched the pilot's frown deepen in the rearview mirror.

"*I don't care*," the pilot spat.

He looked at the woman like she'd lost her mind.

"*I'm* not going out there—"

The woman interrupted the pilot, holding a chipped fingernail to her lips as a fuzzy voice broke through the static of her walkie-talkie. "Joy," the voice said, crackling so loudly that Alejo could hear it without straining. "Finally. It's the president's office. She wants a situation report, and you're the closest to the situation."

Joy smiled at the pilot.

"It's the *president*," she mouthed.

The pilot shook his head in disbelief but grudgingly opened his door—climbing down from the cockpit onto the trembling grass. Joy leaned out into the rain, calling after him as her contact on the walkie-talkie patched her through to Washington.

"Five minutes," she shouted. "No more, okay?"

Alejo grinned and turned in his seat, giving Emily and Elliot a thumbs-up with his good hand. The *president* of the *United States* had tracked them down to see how they were doing . . . but nobody else seemed to care. Elliot was still asleep, his skinny legs splayed out across the cabin, and Emily was sitting very still with her backpack on her lap, looking like she was going to puke or cry.

Or both.

But Alejo wasn't worried, not anymore.

Not with Joy in the cockpit.

—

Joy scraped the polish from her nails as the helicopter's windows fogged.

The first wave of the storm was passing overhead, and she was all alone.

All alone . . . with three bruised kids dripping in the cabin.

She rubbed a hole into the fogged glass and shivered, wishing Rob had found the kids the first time around—before he evacuated, empty-handed, with the rest of the team. Wishing she'd had more of a search party to send in the first place—that the "alpha squad of the NCRC" hadn't been too sick to help. She was up against the clock, and every step of the way, circumstances had been working against her.

The flu, the exhaustion, and the storm—so far ahead of schedule.

So much bigger than they could have ever predicted.

And now that she had the missing kids, their parents were nowhere to be found.

"Typical," she muttered, peering into the rain.

There was no question about it; they'd overstayed their welcome—and the storm was only getting worse. But Joy couldn't leave. Not yet. Five minutes wasn't long enough to sweep the park. Not even on a clear day. And the tremors were intensifying—imperceptibly at first, but the longer they waited, the more the grass started to buckle and shift. Joy could feel it, rolling beneath their skids. There was always *some* seismic activity with BDDs—that was simple physics—but before today, Joy never thought a hurricane could ever be strong enough to cause an actual earthquake.

She just didn't think it was possible.

The president's office had called to confirm that it was.

Before she'd lost the signal, they'd told her to get out as quickly as possible.

"Godspeed," they'd said, their voices crackling and fading in the storm.

Joy hadn't been able to find an active frequency since she'd heard the news.

She chewed on the end of a ragged nail, biting it down to the raw nerves underneath. Every second felt like a lifetime in the tiny helicopter and she didn't want to leave without the parents. She hated the thought of it, but she wouldn't have a choice—not if the pilot and the cameraman came back empty-handed, too. "Come *on*," Joy said, picking up her walkie-talkie and flipping through the channels.

Praying for an open frequency.

"This is Joy Harrison," she whispered, not wanting to scare the kids. "Can anyone hear me?"

Static filled her ears and she turned to face the kids as

she waited for an answer. The boy with the bloodstained shirt was curled into himself, out cold—his cheek resting heavily against the shoulder strap of his seat belt. The other boy was smiling to himself with his eyes closed, his arm swelling on his lap. Only the girl met Joy's eyes, her expectant face wreathed in mud. Joy smiled encouragingly.

But there was no reply.

"I'll be back in two minutes," she said, unable to wait any longer.

She bit her lip and opened the door of the cockpit, slapping the side of the helicopter for good luck as she jumped lightly onto the waterlogged lawn.

"I promise, okay?"

The girl nodded, watching Joy jog into the darkness.

TENT CITY

Emily didn't like waiting in the helicopter, and she definitely didn't like being left alone with Elliot and Alejo—not after everything they'd been through. Not with Elliot so hurt and so helpless. The rain slashed against the thin aluminum hull, hard enough that she could barely hear her own anxious thoughts as they bounced around her head.

Joy *looked* young, she told herself, but she was with the government.

She knew what she was doing.

Or at least, Emily hoped she did, because there was no way she was going to leave her brother again. Not with the city so dark and the wind screaming through the trees. She swallowed, checking Elliot's phone for what felt like the hundredth time. There was still no reception, so she wiped another hole in the window's fog with the palm of her hand and leaned her forehead against the glass.

Keeping her eyes peeled for her parents.

Emily knew she was supposed to stay put, but it felt wrong, not searching for them with everyone else. They were *her* parents, and she couldn't stand the thought of them outside in the storm. Looking for her and her brother. The window fogged over again as Emily sighed. A flash of lightning forked through the trees while she wiped it clean, casting the park in a sickly pink light. In the split second after it struck, Emily saw movement out of the corner of her eye.

Elliot's phone slipped from her fingers, clattering to the grated metal floor.

Momentarily forgotten.

"Look," Emily said, quietly at first and then again, louder ... shaking Alejo by the shoulder. Startled, he clutched his wrist against his chest and then joined her at the window, staring in horror at the black puddles deepening on the lawn. They drowned the clovers and the dandelions in seconds, blanketing the park until there was nothing to see except dark ripples coursing around the helicopter's skids. Emily watched them flow over the trembling grass, racing toward the sinkhole that was quickly forming on the avenue.

She opened her mouth to speak, but no words came out.

Emily closed her mouth and tried again.

But she was speechless.

Blinking in disbelief, she watched the widening hole swallow the heavy stone fountain at the front of the park and the green metal statue that topped it. For a moment, she thought she could hear the fountain's blackened pennies clattering as they fell into the abyss, but it was just the rain. It was coming down much harder now, and the floodwater swelled as it channeled across the field, carrying an abandoned police car in its newfound current. The police car groaned, spinning in slow motion as the houses that lined the park tilted toward the sinkhole, their porches creaking—teetering like dominoes on the verge of collapse.

But not falling.

Not yet.

Emily squinted into the darkness, her hands shaking as she watched the sinkhole spread. The asphalt crumbled like corn bread as it worked its way up the avenue, swallowing sidewalks and streetlights. Time seemed to stretch while thunder rolled overhead, lightning strobing across the nightmarish sky while thin rivulets of white water cascaded into the ragged hole. Alejo and Emily stared at each other, mouths agape, as the rear wheels of the police car tipped beneath the surface of the grass. Its horn blared as it backflipped into the sodden depths, then quieted, muffled by water and distance.

In the ensuing silence, it was easy to believe the worst was over.

But the worst was just beginning.

Forty-five miles beneath the sinking streets, long-dormant tectonic systems had been activated by Valerie's seismic blasts. Prehistoric sediments shifted along forgotten fault lines, grinding against each other as the megastorm worked its way inevitably inland. By the time the bulk of the storm reached the park, the park would be gone—swallowed whole by an earthquake the likes of which the city had never seen. The helicopter bucked—gently at first, and then harder—as the grass pitched beneath its skids.

Emily hooked her arm through the nylon webbing for support, eyeing the cockpit as the cabin rattled. Even if she knew how to fly it, the dashboard was dark and the keys were missing from the ignition.

Without the pilot, they were trapped.

"We have to go," she said, her voice catching in her throat. But there was nowhere *to* go, and even though he was finally awake, Elliot was in no condition to run.

Emily's legs turned to rubber as the helicopter bounced, then spun another half foot toward the sinkhole.

They didn't have a choice.

"We can't stay here."

As if to prove her point, an ancient oak crashed to the ground just inches from the helicopter. Its upper branches exploded through the windshield, showering glass across the cockpit as the cabin filled with leaves and rain and splintered wood. Outside, a woman screamed. Emily's stomach dropped as she picked herself up from the floor. The scream was so twisted with pain that she wished she hadn't recognized it—that she didn't know, instinctively, who it belonged to—but Emily couldn't help it. The woman's voice was a version of her own, just older.

And in trouble.

"Mom!" she shouted.

She didn't want to leave Elliot again—but she couldn't leave her mother, either. Not now. Not with the park eating everything in its path. Elliot's lips pursed, like he was trying not to puke, but he looked at his sister and nodded.

Alejo nodded, too, throwing his good arm around her brother's shoulders.

"Go," he said. "I've got him."

The helicopter twisted another half foot as Emily flung the door open, her wet hair catching in the wind.

She didn't believe the new kid—not a hundred percent, not with the city caving in beneath their feet—but she didn't have a choice. "I'll be back," she said, jumping to the ground. The earth danced beneath her feet as she sprinted alongside the splintered trunk, toward the sound of her mother crying.

It almost felt like the storm was carrying her through the growing darkness.

Like she was flying.

MEGASTORM VALERIE

NEW ORLEANS

JUNE 11—3:37 P.M.

Emily's hair whipped against her face as she slid her hand along the fallen tree, tracing its bark down to its massive roots. Splintered branches scraped her legs and floodwater rushed over her shoes, tugging on her laces as it coursed toward the sinkhole. Half blind from the wind and the rain, it was all Emily could do to keep her eyes open as she followed the fading echoes of her mother's scream.

"Mom!" she shouted, squinting into the storm. "It's me, Emily!"

She stumbled forward, climbing over the debris—kicking and pushing it out of her way until her bruised shins connected with something soft and warm. Something yielding. Emily shrieked, covering her mouth with her trembling hands as she peered down into the dark water at her feet . . . *and gasped.*

It was Joy.

She was on her hands and knees, blood streaming down her cheeks as she dug her chipped blue fingernails into the sludge, clawing herself back to the helicopter through the rising waters. Joy's pupils dilated as she stared back up at Emily, shaking from the shock. The tree weighed thousands of pounds, and some part of it had clipped her as it fell.

That much was obvious.

Swallowing a sudden nausea, Emily propped herself against the closest limb and pulled Joy to her feet. Joy swayed in the wind, blinking as the rain mixed with the blood in her matted hair. It ran down her arms in rivulets, and Emily tried not to gag as Joy hooked her elbow around her narrow shoulders for support.

It was hard to tell how hurt she was in the rain.

But Joy was lucky.

She was alive.

Beyond the roots of the dying tree, the park had collapsed in on itself again.

Emily shuddered as she realized how close they were to the precipice of another gaping sinkhole. It was so vast it had claimed an entire *grove* of ancient trees, and

Emily stood, frozen—twenty feet from its crumbling lips—as the last of them smashed and clattered into the darkness. Centuries of growth, gone in an instant. Only the one oak remained, its gnarled branches speared so deeply into the dirt that it was anchored, immune to the pull of the yawning pit.

"We should've . . . ," Joy mumbled, distracted by the leaves swirling in the current at her feet. They were racing inevitably downward, into the fractures and fault lines vibrating beneath the city. "We should've been gone by now."

The sinkhole creaked and groaned in response, swelling with floodwater.

Expanding.

Emily steered Joy farther into the grounded canopy, hiding from the wind as it ripped the outer branches loose. The sinkhole might have felled the tree, but its thick layers of leaves still blocked the rain, muffling the storm as they pressed deeper into the twisted boughs. Slowing the downpour to a drizzle. Emily stopped to catch her breath, wiping her face dry with the back of her hand. *Listening.* In the strange quiet beneath the shivering leaves, she could hear voices.

They weren't alone.

"Do you think . . ." Emily trailed off, pricking her ears.

"Do you think you can make it to the helicopter without me?"

"I think so," Joy said, stepping backward to test her balance. She leaned against the bark to steady herself as Emily hitched her legs over the mossy trunk. "But I can't just leave you here. . . ."

"It's okay," Emily said, disappearing into the foliage. "I'll be right behind you."

She ducked beneath fallen branches, digging her way through an endless tangle of twigs as she tunneled inward. They scratched at her face and shirt, but Emily didn't have the time to clear a path through the tree. Not with the earth shifting beneath her feet and the sinkholes swallowing everything they touched. The sky flashed pink as lightning forked overhead, casting long-fingered shadows across the drowning park.

Illuminating Emily's mother.

She stood motionless, surrounded by broken greenery in the heart of fallen oak, so sick with fear and worry that her chest convulsed with it. The terrible knot in Emily's stomach finally loosened as she ran into her open arms. "I didn't know," her mother whispered, clenching Emily into a hug so tight she could feel it in her ribs. She sobbed softly, her cheeks wet against Emily's forehead—whether from rain or blood or tears, Emily couldn't tell. *"I didn't know,"* her mother repeated, so quietly it was barely a whisper. Her face crumpled as she tucked a muddy strand of tangled hair behind Emily's ear, but their reunion was short-lived. The tree shook all around them—suddenly and violently, showering them with acorns and Spanish moss—and Emily shrugged free from their embrace.

"Wait," her mother said, *"Emily—"*

But there wasn't time to talk.

There was barely time to think.

Emily pulled her mother's wrist, dragging her through the twigs and brambles. Pushing her—when her mom dug her heels into the mud—toward the waiting helicopter. They were so close that Emily could see it through the leaves, glinting brightly as the lightning flashed, and she couldn't understand why her mom wasn't trying harder to reach it.

"Emily!" her mom shouted, wresting her arm free.

She pointed back into the thick of the fallen tree.

Emily blinked the rain from her eyes, twisting her head in the direction of her mother's finger . . . and ran, her voice lost in the thunder as she shouted for her dad. His shirt was ripped and stained with grass and mud, his muscles straining as he pushed against a tangle of branches. Yelling from the effort. The oak tree groaned, but not because he'd moved it. The dirt beneath its roots was caving in, dragging the tree—inch by terrifying inch—into the depths of the sinkhole.

Pulling her father down with it.

"Dad!" Emily shouted. "We have to go!"

Lifting himself from the thickening mud, Emily's father shook his head. Rain cascaded down his face as he grasped the mossy branches, but he didn't move to wipe his brow. He shouted into the storm instead, pushing his shoulder against the bark as he tried to right the fallen oak. "Dad!" Emily yelled, reaching for his sweaty arm. "It's me!"

But her father just kept lifting, his jaw clenched from the effort.

"Don't look!" he grunted, straining against the wreckage of the tree.

But it was too late.

Emily's heart stopped as the floodwaters puddled over the awkwardly splayed legs of the pilot, who was pinned to the ground beneath a heavy limb. His face was contorted into a grimace, but he wasn't moving. Not even as the dark water lapped against the side of his head, threatening to suck him deeper into the mud beneath their feet. The cameraman groaned at the pilot's side, knocked unconscious by the very same branch—but not trapped.

Not yet.

Emily's mother screamed.

"No," Emily whispered.

Without the pilot, they didn't have a chance.

She splashed beneath the heavy branch, pushing against its bark with every muscle in her body, and collapsed to her knees when the tree failed to move. Not even an inch. Thunder crashed overhead and mud streamed down Emily's face as she crawled through the water, bracing her feet against the tree for leverage as she tugged at the pilot's arms. She pulled so hard she was sure she was going hurt him, but he didn't budge. She would have given up if both of his hands weren't fists, clenched so tightly she was sure that he was still alive.

That they could still save him and get to the helicopter in time.

Emily tightened her grip on the pilot's balled fists, pulling him with all her strength as the first house toppled on the avenue. The screech of wrenching wood and metal cut through the rain like the cry of a wounded animal and the cameraman moaned at her feet, clutching his temples as its beams and shingles clattered into the shivering earth.

Yielding to the storm.

"One more time," Emily's dad grunted, launching himself at the giant branch as aftershocks rippled through the park. The tree jerked backward as he wrestled against it, unmoored at the edge of oblivion by the swelling tremors. Limbs snapped—ripped and smashed from its trunk—as the tree rolled away from the pilot, crashing farther into the sinkhole.

Finally free, the pilot relaxed, unfolding his fist in Emily's hand.

In the center of his dirty palm, silver and shining, was a small metal key.

Emily wiped the key clean on her ragged shirt while her dad staggered under the weight of the injured pilot.

"Okay," he said, nudging the woozy cameraman with the toe of his boot. "Let's go."

FIVE HUNDRED FEET AND COUNTING ABOVE NEW ORLEANS

JUNE 11—3:46 P.M.

Emily cleared the controls with the back of her arm, sweeping chunks of shatterproof glass and splintered wood to the floor of the cockpit. Her heart pounded as she tried to find the ignition. It didn't help that the upper branches of the ancient oak were still poking through the windshield, pulling against the helicopter as the tree shuddered and slipped farther beneath the surface of the park. Rain filtered down through its leaves, dripping onto a hundred switches and gauges that flickered to life as Emily turned the tiny, silver key in the dash.

Outside the helicopter, she could hear the sinkholes expanding.

Pulling the rest of the avenue into their depths.

Swallowing everything they touched.

But Emily didn't have time to look.

"Now what?" she shouted, glancing up from the blinking controls as her dad climbed into the cabin. He stumbled beneath the weight of the injured pilot, gently dropping him into the copilot's chair at Emily's side. Emily looked back and forth between her dad and the pilot for instructions, but none were forthcoming. The pilot just groaned, grasping at his broken legs as her dad climbed back into the cabin. Sobbing, Emily's mom clutched Elliot to her chest as she watched her husband dig through the cargo holds, hunting for a first-aid kit. He tossed three bright orange life vests onto the metal grating, then a flare gun. Finally, he ripped open a small white box, unspooling the skinny roll of gauze inside and throwing it to the ground in frustration. It wasn't enough to cover the wounds on the pilot's thigh.

It wouldn't stop the bleeding.

"We need to get him fixed enough to *fly* this thing," her dad shouted, pulling his button-down shirt over his head. He climbed back into the cockpit in his undershirt, kicking the first-aid kit as he knelt beside Emily. He wrapped his own torn sleeves above the pilot's knee, pulling them as tightly as he could. The pilot screamed, spittle running down his chin. But Emily's dad kept pulling, cinching the makeshift tourniquet into a sloppy knot.

Emily twisted in her chair, averting her eyes.

But the backseat had its problems, too.

The cameraman had collapsed on the bench between Joy and Alejo, and the three of them were so bruised and bloody that Emily winced just looking at them. "How's it going up there?" the cameraman slurred, stroking mud from his scraggly beard as Alejo nursed his wrist. Even the headset dangling from Joy's neck was broken, its connection to the president's office severed along with the telephone wires on the avenue.

They were alone, Emily realized.

They were alone and nobody was coming to save them.

"Are we ready to go now?" Emily asked, turning back to the pilot.

He grimaced at the sound of her voice, shrinking farther into his seat.

Emily's dad frowned at his side, waiting for the pilot's pain to subside while Emily stared at the dashboard. She tried to read the gauges, but they didn't make sense. There was no button to make the helicopter fly, no gas pedal to stomp. She jiggled the joystick between her knees and could feel that *something* was happening overhead, but when she craned her neck to check if the blades were spinning, all she could see was the roiling black core of Megastorm Valerie, towering just blocks away. Emily pulled the joystick harder, squeezing its red trigger over and over and over again.

Panicking.

But still, nothing happened.

The helicopter wasn't moving.

"He *has* to help us!" she shouted, shaking her dad by the shoulder. Making him drop the aspirin he'd salvaged from the tiny kit. Before he could answer, the flood-waters surged, slamming them against the dashboard. Emily fumbled with her shoulder straps, locking them into place—*better late than never*—as the helicopter slid another ten feet toward the growing sinkhole. . . .

Wrenching itself from the fallen oak with a crash.

Valerie's headwinds roared through the broken windshield, filling the cabin like a parachute as the last of the helicopter's windows showered to the floor. The ground beneath their skids pulsed with tremors and the cameraman braced himself against the nylon webbing—but there was nothing for Emily to brace herself against as she stared into the encroaching darkness, face to face with Megastorm Valerie. She reached across the narrow aisle, tapping frantically on the pilot's arm.

Help, she mouthed.

Drawn and white, the pilot didn't answer.

"Go, go, go," Emily's mom shouted from the backseat as her dad leaned closer to the pilot, repeating simple yes-or-no questions in the hopes that the pilot might nod or shake his head. That he might give them *any* kind of clue that would help get the helicopter off the ground. "Do I push a button to make the rotors start?" her dad asked, his voice as level and soft as the storm was wild. The pilot just trembled in his seat, his face distorted in agony. Emily's dad nodded, then gestured at a quadrant of flashing lights on the dashboard.

"Is it one of *these* buttons?"

Emily couldn't wait any longer.

She slapped the dashboard, running her fingers across the toggles and switches.

Flipping them randomly.

Praying for movement.

But nothing happened.

"Come on," she whispered. *"Go."*

The temperature cooled as the churning eyewall of Megastorm Valerie approached, so quickly that the hair on Emily's arms stood on end. With the cold front came a fresh wave of rain. It fell hard and fast, lightning striking on all sides as thunder enveloped the helicopter.

Emily shivered, shocked into a momentary deafness.

Her ears rang as the fault lines beneath the streets rumbled in response, the cockpit rolling and swaying beneath her feet. Swallowing her fear, she squinted at the glowing gauges as the helicopter spun slowly and deliberately toward the avenue, carried by rising wavelets that splashed roughly against its battered metal frame. The sky had grown so dark—and so suddenly—that Emily could barely see the sinkholes anymore.

But she could feel them.

They all could.

She squeezed her eyes shut as the helicopter shifted again, jumping another few feet toward the hole. "Snap out of it!" her dad shouted at the pilot, losing his calm as the entire cabin tumbled forward in a tangle of limbs: arms and legs and wordless shouts, all slamming into the back of the captain's chair. Alejo yelped, his bad wrist pinned painfully beneath Elliot in the pileup. Emily joined him, screaming as the nose of the helicopter dipped precariously over the void.

"You have to help us!" she yelled.

She yelled it again and again, so loudly and at such a high pitch that the pilot frowned—shaken, finally, from his stupor. Fighting gravity and his own broken body, he ran his fingers along the side of Emily's chair, feeling for a familiar lever. He screamed as he pulled it, the tendons in his neck popping from the effort—and then he collapsed, slouching against the windowless door.

At first, it felt like nothing happened.

The wind shrieked across the chasm so piercingly that Emily could hear it above the ringing in her ears—but she couldn't hear the rotors humming into action above her head. It was only when the joystick started shaking in her white-knuckled fist that she dared to open her eyes again. Gathering the last of her courage, she looked down into the sinkhole and blinked the wind from her widening eyes. She was still staring over the edge of the abyss. . . .

But they weren't falling.

They were floating above it, shooting skyward so quickly that Emily's stomach jumped into her throat as she peered into the floodwaters—watching them shrink beneath her dripping-wet shoes. Emily's dad joined her in the captain's chair as they rose, wrapping his calloused hands around hers on the joystick. Steadying it as wind-blown debris pinged the sides of the helicopter so hard it dented the metal frame and pierced straight through the tortured chassis. In the rearview mirror, Emily could see her mother hugging Elliot and Alejo, squeezing them tightly as hot tears streaked Emily's cheeks.

But it wasn't time to cry.

Not yet.

Not with the black expanse of Megastorm Valerie filling the broken windshield.

Emily wiped her cheeks with the back of her hand as the helicopter strained against the storm's outer winds, its rotors whining from the struggle. Her dad pulled the pilot's lever even harder and the engine keened, shooting them higher into the sky above the park. They twisted in the updrafts, spinning faster and faster—and the joystick jumped in Emily's palm, bucking her grip. When she couldn't hold it any longer, she simply let go. She didn't like ceding control to the storm, but they were running out of time and there was no use fighting it.

Valerie was too strong, and the only way out . . .

Was up.

Rain blasted through the broken windshield, stinging Emily's cheeks as they spiraled out of control. The world outside the helicopter blended into grays and blacks and blues, and Emily saw Alejo dry-heave in the rearview mirror. It was the last thing she remembered seeing before her dad pulled her into a tight hug, sheltering her from the crosswinds as they twisted through the writhing cloudbanks and into the thinning upper reaches of the storm.

"Hold tight," someone yelled.

Emily hunched over, tucking her head into her lap as the rotors started to smoke.

Out of the corner of her eyes, she could see the city

below them. It was whirling like the floor of a carousel, a point of spinning focus at the center of an endless blur. She stared into the shrinking park as they spun, watching the first surge of storm water run through deep fissures in the earth, filling the gaps between the trees that were still standing.

Swallowing her tiny island.

Emily squeezed her eyes shut, tears cutting through the mud on her cheeks as the helicopter continued to rise—its body shaking as it climbed over three thousand feet above sea level, and then six thousand. At ten thousand feet, they finally broke free from the worst of the storm. With the highest winds safely beneath them, the helicopter slowed into a gentle spin, looping in arabesques above the darkened city.

"Look," Alejo said.

From so high up, everything was small.

The park, the highways, even the spinning mass of the megastorm.

As they drifted upward through the gathering clouds, surfing a trailing wind, lightning flashed beneath them—harmless, like fireflies. Emily took one deep breath and then another, staring into the rearview mirror as she recovered from the shock. Joy and the cameraman leaned into their shoulder straps, staring—like Alejo—into the darkness below while her brother rested against the curve of her mother's neck. Emily sighed, exhaling as she felt her backpack rustle at her feet. She frowned at first, then smiled as she unzipped it. Her turtle was still in her bag. He'd finally come out of his shell again and was chewing the corner of her book.

It was thick with mud and spackled with algae.

But Emily had bigger things to worry about.

"Where are we going now?" she asked, her cheeks red from the wind as she leaned back into the crook of her father's arm. He shifted to make room for her, replacing his hand on the helicopter's joystick with her own. She held it lightly, letting the currents guide her as she kept one eye on her turtle and the other on her brother in the rearview mirror.

"We can figure that out later," her dad said. "For now, let's just fly."

TEN THOUSAND FEET AND COUNTING ABOVE THE MISSISSIPPI RIVER

JUNE 11—5:52 P.M.

The turtle contracted his neck, pulling his head back into his mossy shell. He blinked sleepily as his thick skin folded up around his ears, warming his cold blood and muffling the wind. He hated the way it whistled, unceasingly, across the lip of his carapace, but there was only so long he could hide. And there was so much happening outside his shell that he didn't understand. As soon as the helicopter leveled out above the storm, he sniffed—stretching his wrinkled neck back out into the cockpit.

Sensing movement, the girl hugged him tightly against her chest.

He struggled against her grip, pushing into her arms with his webbed claws. He didn't *want* to scratch her, but he was curious—and the girl wasn't going to put him down without a fight.

"We'll just follow the river," her father said. "Do you see it, that brown squiggle down there?" The girl traced the curve of the Mississippi River with her fingers and the turtle opened his beak, threating to snap at them as he wriggled against her shirt.

"Fine," the girl mumbled, setting him down at her feet. Too distracted to deal with him.

The turtle smiled to himself, testing the air with the tip of his tongue as he followed his nose into the cabin. The hard metal grating shook through his stout little legs, vibrating him to his very core as he scrambled beneath the fold-down seats, taking experimental nibbles at wet shoelaces and the hems of waterlogged jeans. But none of them were as satisfying as the girl's old book, with its soft paper marinated so nicely in algae and dirt. Undeterred, the turtle traced its scent all the way back into her backpack, the nub of his tail wagging expectantly behind him.

"Can you set down there?" the girl's father shouted, pointing to a light green patch beyond the empty windshield. The pilot nodded as the girl helped her father transfer him into the captain's chair, but the turtle was too busy chewing to notice.

"Do we have enough gas?"

"Barely," the pilot said, sucking his teeth as the girl positioned his muddy shoes on the pedals beneath the dash. Tailwinds had pushed them upward and out of danger, but the helicopter wouldn't fly without fuel . . . and it had quickly become clear that the injured pilot was the only person who could set them down safely. He puffed his cheeks out as he wrapped his ashen hands around the controls.

"Here goes nothing," he whispered, his voice cracking in the wind.

With the pilot back where he belonged, the girl was free to search the cabin for her runaway turtle. She checked beneath the seats and in the emptied cargo holds behind the legs of her sleeping friends. The turtle, happily munching on the corners of his book, was oblivious. It wasn't until the girl strapped herself in between her mother and the boy with the broken wrist that she finally lifted her backpack onto her lap. She squeezed it to her chest as the helicopter began its jerking descent.

"There you are," she said, grinning as she reached to pet his knobby head.

The turtle opened his beak, startled by the shift in pressure.

But he didn't snap at the girl's fingers.

He closed his eyes instead, nuzzling against her open palm as the helicopter jumped down through the clouds.

OXFORD, MISSISSIPPI

JUNE 11—7:45 P.M.

The entire cabin shook as the pilot wrestled the wind with the last of his fading strength. He'd managed to slow their approach, but just barely. The helicopter was falling too fast to settle down in a gentle hover, and the rotors screamed overhead—overworked and running on fumes. Alejo bit into the thick weave of his shoulder strap as they hurtled toward a small patch of mottled green, losing altitude so quickly that he felt his stomach pushing at the back of his throat.

After everything they'd been through, it didn't seem fair that they could crash.

Please, he thought, clenching his teeth.

Thinking of his mother and Padrino Nando.

Please let us live through this.

Emily's mom wrapped her arm around his shoulders and clutched him alongside her own son, shouting wordlessly into their ears as the cabin lights blinked off and on again. For a second, Alejo felt weightless. But just for a second. He watched the orange life vests float upward, tapping the roof of the helicopter before slamming back down to the floor.

It was faster to fall than to land, he realized. . . .

But not in time to brace himself before their narrow skids connected with the earth. The seat belt dug into his shoulder, his arms and legs flailing as the shock from the impact rippled through the helicopter's thin metal frame. Alejo could hear it crumple as it bounced. He could *feel* it twisting and tearing as the helicopter's nose tapped down into the dirt, bucking him against his harness while it slid to a scraping stop.

Emily gripped Alejo's swollen hand, squeezing it tightly in her trembling fingers.

For once, Alejo didn't flinch.

The pain didn't even register.

Back on terra firma, the helicopter continued to shake, its engine buckling, its blades angled dangerously close to the ground. Alejo stared at their spinning shadows on the grass outside the broken windows. Too stunned to move. Somebody coughed, and the pilot collapsed in the captain's chair as Alejo finally unclipped his seat belt. He staggered toward the door, his good hand pressed against his temple as he stepped into a bright summer evening. Behind him, the rest of the cabin began to stir. The cameraman untangled himself from the nylon webbing and Joy tapped her broken headset, praying for a signal. Even Emily's backpack jostled in her lap, her turtle stretching through the open flap.

Blinking at the wreckage.

But Alejo didn't look back—only forward.

The sky was bright pink and periwinkle blue, clear enough that he could see the moon starting to shine above him even as the sun melted into the horizon. Clusters of streetlamps hung from wrought-iron poles, casting the lower limbs of budding crepe myrtle trees in a soft amber glow. Alejo spun in a slow circle, his heart still pounding in his chest as he checked for storm clouds.

"Alejo!" the cameraman shouted, limping out of the helicopter.

Alejo squinted into the sunset.

They'd crash-landed in the middle of a university, and not a small one.

The grounds were well mowed and manicured, surrounded on all sides by stately redbrick buildings topped with bright white spires. A loose circle of college students had gathered around the helicopter. They slouched beneath the weight of their backpacks, their fruit smoothies and Frisbees long forgotten as they held up their phones to film Alejo and the blades that were still spinning. . . .

Alejo closed his eyes.

His blood pounded in his ears and his knees shook, even though he was on firm ground again. It wasn't until the cameraman joined him, resting his arm heavily on the top of his head, that the world seemed to snap back into focus. The whir of the helicopter's engine had turned into a ratcheting clank and the circle of students had widened—jumping back onto the sidewalk as Alejo's new friends helped their dad carry the injured pilot to the grass. In the distance, sirens cut through the soft blanket of the settling twilight.

"Hey," one of the students said. "Are you okay?"

Alejo shook his head clear as the cameraman squeezed his shoulder, then sat cross-legged at his feet. "We're okay," the cameraman said, rolling back onto the grass and laughing—rough and wild, his arms stretched wide in either direction. A knot on his head bulged above his muddy beard, blue and yellow and sickly green.

"Kid, we made it—we're okay!"

Alejo nodded, gesturing to borrow the young woman's phone.

It was still filming, and Alejo smiled weakly into the

lens as she handed it to him. "Just for a second," he said, reaching into his pocket for the folded note his *padrino* had left him back in La Perla. The paper was torn, the ink smudged from the rain, but Alejo smoothed its creases as he broke through the buzzing circle of students— rubbing the postscript with the pad of his thumb as he walked beneath the trees and the glowing streetlamps.

Dialing the phone number Padrino Nando had scrawled in the margins.

In case we get separated, the old man had written.

Alejo recognized the number, but it didn't belong to his *padrino.*

There had been no point to call it before, while he was running from the storm. But now, with the helicopter smoldering on the lawn behind him, Alejo held the student's phone to his ear. He took a deep breath as fire engines roared onto the campus and the red, flashing lights of three ambulances danced against the trees.

Covering his ears, he stared down at his shoes— waiting for the phone to ring.

"Hi," Alejo said. "Mamá?"

THREE DAYS LATER

AFTERWARD

SAN JUAN, PUERTO RICO

JUNE 14—7:30 A.M.

Padrino Nando picked his way through the wreckage, sipping a hot *café con leche* out of a wax paper cup, the morning's newspaper folded beneath his arm. He'd caught an early bus down to the city to check on La Perla and was happy to see that it hadn't been washed out to sea like the newscasters said—not completely, anyway.

But it wasn't home anymore.

His little yellow house was roofless and covered in a thin layer of silt.

He could see it from the top of the wall and had wanted to get closer, to inspect the damage, but the concrete stairs leading down into the neighborhood were impassable. At least for him. There were footprints in the mud where some of his neighbors had slid through the rubble, but Nando was content to let his house sit in the sun and dry without him.

At least for a while.

The beach had calmed since the last time he'd seen it.

The water was glassy, the sky so bright it hurt his eyes.

Drawn to a crew of workers and their portable radio, he stepped carefully over a downed power line—giving a wide berth to emergency trailers and white FEMA tents as he took the scenic route to the sun-dazzled waves. The salty breeze cooled his coffee as he walked, his flip-flops sinking into the sand while the workers tossed driftwood and frayed nets onto mounds of beach trash. Children shouted, chasing each other through the cleanup as a local jazz station mingled with the soft wash of surf.

Reminding Padrino Nando of Alejo.

He sat on an overturned shopping cart and smiled.

The boy would be back sooner or later, visiting with his mother—and Padrino Nando was determined for his house to be rebuilt and waiting for them, ready for whenever they returned. He set his drink in the sand and snapped the newspaper open across his lap, scanning the headlines. They were all sad, of course.

It broke Nando's heart to read them.

Valerie had done her worst from San Juan all the way to St. Louis, Missouri (MISSISSIPPI RIVER JUMPS BANKS).

People were hurt (HUNDREDS INJURED IN BRIDGE COL-LAPSE) and people were stranded (MEGASTORM LEAVES THOUSANDS HOMELESS). It was hard to imagine a time when the world would be healed again.

But Padrino Nando has hopeful.

Like the workers on the beach, there were people helping everywhere he looked. They were giving time and food, and money when they could. They were re-building what the storm had taken. Nando folded the newspaper shut and dropped it at his side, sipping his coffee as the gulls circled overhead. It wasn't until he'd finished that he heard the little bird chirping at his feet.

Nando's joints creaked as he leaned over to investi-gate.

Beneath his newspaper, wrapped tightly in a tattered plastic bag, was a little storm-worn petrel half buried in the sand. His beady eyes darted left and right as Nando dug him free, cradling the half-drowned bird in his wrin-kled hands. But when he set the bird down in front of him, untangled and free to fly away, the bird didn't move.

It just stared at him.

Padrino Nando patted his pockets, feeling for the tin of fish he'd been saving for lunch. *Anchovies in mustard.* The bird cocked his head as he peeled the tin open, wip-ing the spicy mustard from the fish on his pants and toss-ing the first anchovy into the sand.

"Hola, amigo," Nando said, feeding the little bird another piece of fish, and another, until the tin was empty. A thin metal band on the little bird's leg flashed in the morning light as Nando took out his new cell phone—a necessity, he had decided, in these troubling times. While the petrel pecked at the mustard in the empty tin, he took a picture to send to Alejo's mom.

To show Alejo that the birds were back.

Just like he'd promised they would be.

"He's a lucky one," Padrino Nando typed. "He made it through the storm."

Realizing there were no more fish, the petrel stretched and stumbled toward the sea. By the time Padrino's message reached Alejo and his mother, the little bird was airborne, circling with the gulls overhead as the sun dipped behind a passing cloud. A new song came on the radio and the beach workers turned up the volume as Nando squinted at the petrel's silhouette. Behind him, on the mainland, he could hear trucks backing up and hammers banging. It hadn't been a week and already La Perla was starting to rise up around him, like a phoenix from the watery ashes.

He watched the little bird swoop down to the surface of the ocean.

He skimmed the waves with his long black legs—so happy to be alive that he could barely contain himself—

then soared back up above the clouds. Padrino Nando stood up and shielded his eyes, smiling as the petrel flew into the sunrise. He kept staring even after the little bird disappeared, an unexpected tear running down his weathered face as he noticed that the clouds on the horizon weren't silver-lined, like the saying said.

They were golden.

Author's Note

According to the Hurricane Research Division of the National Oceanic and Atmospheric Administration (NOAA), an average of thirteen tropical storms and hurricanes make their way through the Atlantic Ocean every year. As I'm writing this note, the NOAA is predicting up to sixteen named storms (storms big enough to warrant a name, like Valerie) and as many as four major hurricanes during the 2018 season.

There's a tropical storm headed for New Orleans right now.

It's working its way up into the Gulf of Mexico from the Caribbean, ruining a long summer weekend with storm surge warnings and flash flood advisories. I know because my mom called to tell me that her plans had been rained out—but other than that, she didn't sound too worried about the storm. They're so frequent on the Gulf Coast that they're easy to ignore.

At least, until they aren't.

My mother isn't originally from New Orleans, but she

moved to Louisiana from Miami, where having a gas-powered oven was a point of pride in her big Italian family (so they could cook hurricane feasts midstorm, even if the power went out). As a first-generation New Orleanian, I grew up not far from Audubon Park. And growing up in New Orleans means growing up with hurricanes. I'm not sure if it was simpler times or if the storms were just weaker then, but I remember playing in the flood-water in the calm eye of a hurricane with the rest of the kids in my neighborhood and standing in high winds, my arms spread wide as gray clouds raced across a strange green and yellow sky.

I moved away from New Orleans before my senior year of high school, and for the next ten years I lived all over the place, from Florida to Indonesia, Boston, Colonial Williamsburg (in Virginia), and Brooklyn, New York. While I was away, Hurricane Katrina hit my hometown—a hurricane so catastrophic it ended up costing over $160 *billion* in damage. I was with friends from home when it happened, friends who ended up living with me while the story unfolded. The phone lines were overloaded, so we watched the news—and as the months wore on, we watched the news coverage shift to the next breaking stories.

There's always something new to report.

But my mother's house was still a wreck, and even

now—over a decade later—New Orleans feels different somehow. The population never fully bounced back after the evacuations, and even though the city has started to look more like its old self, there are still houses that are boarded up in neighborhoods overgrown with vines.

According to researchers at the National Aeronautics and Space Administration (NASA), storms are only getting stronger and more frequent, so it was a shock—but it wasn't a surprise, after I shared an early draft of this book with my agent—to see the news about a major hurricane making landfall in Puerto Rico. The fictional megastorm Valerie passed through San Juan for a reason: it's a major city on an island situated squarely in Hurricane Alley, a section of the Atlantic Ocean (and the Caribbean Sea) where atmospheric conditions are perfect for hurricanes.

It made sense, meteorologically.

I read the news with a sinking feeling.

We often only hear about natural disasters when they affect "us" directly. When a hurricane approaches our shores, it makes national news, but we rarely hear about what happens *before* that same hurricane is within striking distance (except, on occasion, to predict how bad a storm is going to be by the time it reaches our front doors). That's the reason I wanted to write about a hurricane from start to finish, and on a human scale: to really think about the many ways people (and animals!) are affected and connected by these types of storms, despite invisible borders and geographical boundaries. As I followed the news in the days and weeks after the most recent hurricane, I felt that connection so clearly, it was like a flashback. The aftermath in the Caribbean was all too familiar: devastation and heartbreak and the kind of helplessness you feel when a problem is so big it seems impossible to solve. There were calls for charity and governmental intervention; there were heroic first responders and official statements by politicians who felt pressure to weigh in.

And then the news cycle moved inevitably onward.

In its wake, as always, were the people unlucky enough to have been at the mercy of a storm. People like my mom, who found the courage and determination to rebuild their communities from the ground up long after the rest of the world had moved on. Just knowing that it can take months or even years for a region to recover from a natural disaster can feel overwhelming for those of us watching from afar, and it can be hard to know how to help . . . or even where to start. But whether you're a kid or an adult, you can always make a difference in the lives of people affected by a storm.

And you can do it from anywhere.

In fact, unless you're a trained first responder or registered volunteer, it's actually better *not* to show up un-announced in the wake of a natural disaster. In the days and weeks after a hurricane, first responders have their hands full with time-sensitive recovery efforts, so one of the best ways to help is to visit the websites of the local and national relief organizations that are already hard at work in the affected areas, like the American Red Cross or the National Voluntary Organizations Active in Disaster. (Adults can register to volunteer after a natural disaster through the National VOAD website.) Sometimes these organizations will list specific items that are needed, like diapers or baby food—but more often than not, they'll ask you not to send care packages, which can actually slow down recovery efforts. (It might seem like a good idea to mail blankets and canned goods to people in need, but warehouses filled with unmarked boxes can mean a lot of extra work for busy first responders.) Instead, consider organizing a fund-raiser at your school or in your community. In addition to raising awareness about people in need, you'll be making a much-appreciated financial donation.

And it's not just people who need help after a hurricane. Pets are easily separated from their families in the confusion of a storm, and animal shelters can become overcrowded with thousands of homeless dogs and cats in the days and weeks after a hurricane. To make room, these pets are relocated to adoption centers around the country, where they're in real need of care, affection, and—when it's impossible to reunite them with their original families—new homes. So if you're an animal lover, the aftermath of a natural disaster is the perfect time to ask your parent or guardian about adopting a dog or a cat. The American Society for the Prevention of Cruelty to Animals (ASPCA) and the Humane Society are a good source for updates and information about displaced pets following any natural disaster.

While writing this book, I frequently visited the websites of the NOAA, the National Hurricane Center, and the National Weather Service. Readers interested in learning more about hurricanes and other natural disasters should check out the National Weather Service's Young Meteorologist and Owlie Skywarn programs . . . and if you want to see what a hurricane actually looks like, there are about a thousand documentaries to choose from. (These can be hard to watch, but *NOVA*'s "Inside the Megastorm" and "Storm That Drowned a City" are good places to start.)

A word of caution: the more you learn about natural disasters, the more it can seem like there's nothing we can do to stop them—but, to quote the (fictional) National Climatic Research Center, *forewarned is forearmed*. While hurricanes are naturally occurring, some of the smartest scientists and researchers in the world have found that global climate change (in the form of rising ocean temperatures) has increased the strength and intensity of recent storms. Luckily for us, climate change is preventable, and there are hundreds of ways each of us can fight it every day! It can be as simple as planting a tree and remembering to recycle or riding a bike instead of taking a car . . . but caring for our environment—and convincing the adults in our lives to care, too—is the best way to keep our planet healthy.

Turtles and all.

Acknowledgments

This book would not have been possible without the enthusiasm and endless encouragement of my best friend (and literary agent), Rachel Ekstrom Courage—and it's an even better and bigger story than I ever imagined because of the editorial vision of Wendy Loggia and Audrey Ingerson at Delacorte Press.

I'm also forever thankful to all of the booksellers, librarians, authors, and friends who have supported me—especially to Lauren Tarshis, for her generosity in reading an early version of this novel (and for writing pulse-pounding books about survival and resilience with empathy and compassion!).

Very special thanks to Richard and Sandra Ekstrom, patrons of the arts and hosts of Pittsburgh's premier literary incubator—and to my ornithologist sister, Dr. Donata Henry, for being an inspiration (to me and to the world in general); my mother, Adrienne Petrosini, for raising readers and fighting the good fight; and Ben and Ella, for being friends to the animals and giving me hope for the future.

As a New Orleanian, I've seen my fair share of hurricanes ... and hurricane seasons are only getting longer and more unpredictable as our weather systems react to human-induced climate change. I'd like to take this opportunity to thank the scientists, politicians, and activists who continue to advocate for common-sense policies that would protect our planet, as well as the individuals and organizations who jump in and help when natural disasters inevitably strike.

About the Author

Nick Courage is a New Orleans–born writer and aspiring skateboarder who splits his time between Brooklyn and Pittsburgh, where he lives with his wife and two cats. His work has recently appeared in *The Paris Review Daily* and *Writer's Digest*. Follow his adventures on Instagram and Twitter!

nickcourage.com

@nickcourage 🄾

@nickcourage 🐦